THE
MONSTER
OF
ELENDHAVEN

THE
MONSTER
OF
ELENDHAVEN

JENNIFER GIESBRECHT

A TOM DOHERTY ASSOCIATES BOOK

NEW YORK

THE MONSTER OF ELENDHAVEN

Copyright © 2019 by Jennifer Young

Edited by Carl Engle-Laird

A Tor.com Book
Published by Tom Doherty Associates
120 Broadway
New York, NY 10271

www.tor.com

Tor® is a registered trademark of
Macmillan Publishing Group, LLC.

The Library of Congress Cataloging-in-Publication Data
is available upon request.

ISBN 978-1-250-22568-9 (hardcover)
ISBN 978-1-250-22535-1 (ebook)

Our books may be purchased in bulk for promotional, educational,
or business use. Please contact your local bookseller or the
Macmillan Corporate and Premium Sales Department at
1-800-221-7945, extension 5442, or by email at
MacmillanSpecialMarkets@macmillan.com.

First Edition: September 2019

Printed in the United States of America

10   9   8

*To all my friends who believed that I'd get here eventually
even when I didn't: thank you for everything.
You had to listen to a lot of crap.*

THE
MONSTER
OF
ELENDHAVEN

– I –

JOHANN

For a long time, he didn't have a name. What he had were long white fingers that hooked into purses and a mouth that told easy lies. What he had were eyes that remembered faces, feet that knew the alleys, palms that grew calloused and soot stained from crawling through the cobblestone streets.

He got the name when he was three feet and four inches tall, kneeling on the dock with a coin in his palm, from a sailor who stank of rum and fish oil. The sailor grabbed him by the back of the neck and slammed his head into the wall—once, twice, three times—and then yanked the coin from his hand. His lip split on the dock and his mouth filled with a foul mixture of grease, salt, and blood.

"What's your name, then?" the sailor asked, turning the coin to catch the light.

He shook his head, confused. What is a name?

The sailor laughed and kicked him in the ribs. "Why,

don't you have one, dock rat? No little Hans, little Ralf. Little wee Johann of Elendhaven? Nameless spit of a hallankind." The sailor kicked him a second time for good measure. "Suspect I'll find you dead on the shore any day now, beached like a rotten seal."

He put a hand over his mouth and let the spit and blood pool hot and sticky in the center of his palm. "Little Hans," he whispered to himself, "little Ralf." He turned the last one again and again as he wobbled to his feet. "Little Johann, little Johann, a little thing with a little name."

Things with names didn't turn up cracked and ground against the rocky shoreline. Things with names survived. He would be a Thing with a name.

* * *

A creature newly named is a creature still half-animal, and Johann's self-education made generous space for the use of tools and the vice of violence before he could learn regret. He learned lessons like this:

A man wrenching fingers in his hair. Forcing him to the ground. Forcing a lot of other things, too, all the while grunting and pressing bloody little half circles in his shoulders. When it was over Johann was left lying in a puddle of his own sweat and piss, staring at a very large, very sharp rock. Without his thinking about it, his fingers closed around the rock and he stumbled to his feet.

He found the man and kicked him in the nose, bashed his face with the sharp rock, and ground his heel into his windpipe, relishing the muted snap of cartilage and all the delightful little croaks that bubbled up and out of the man's mouth. When the man stopped moving, Johann used the rock on his face until it wasn't a face anymore. He stared at the blood and pressed a stained palm to his heart. He panted heavily, in time with the flutter between his ribs.

Power was sweeter than apples. It was cheaper than water, and sustained the soul twice as well. If Johann was going to be a Thing with a name, then from now on he would be a Thing with power, too.

* * *

Johann grew another three feet so fast his body could hardly keep up. His skin was pallid and thin, stretched taut over a skeleton that threatened to slice through his flesh at every knobby juncture. He walked with a deliberate slouch, arms knifing out from his body at hard angles when he placed them in his pockets. He cultivated a persona with the dedicated fervour of a character actor: a practised charm that appeared natural, a crooked smile, an easy laugh, spider-leg fingers that snapped and threaded through the air as he spoke. The role became so lived-in and claustrophobic that the effort required to peel back the skin was not worth the reveal. He never took his gloves off.

He knew of two ways to make money, and he knew that he didn't like the first one.

He killed to get the things he wanted: a professor of literature's pretty, smiling throat taught him how to read; a seamstress bled to death from a long, craggy gash down the center of her back once she finished the trimming of his jacket. He was careful with her, frog-stitching the overlocked seams of her spine with a boning knife, whistling to himself as he worked. A butcher showed him how to disassemble a body, and then disappeared down the drain in pieces himself. Johann liked killing. He appreciated that every part of the killing act was a function of instinct, that any thinking person is only a breath away from an animal. A half creature with no name.

He refined killing, practised it like an art. He practised like his knife was a horsehair bow being pulled over a throat stringed with catgut. As he grew skilled, he began to live life with the philosophical enthusiasm of a man eating his last meal. He showed up at parties uninvited, drank with the dock rats on holidays, sat in the square at dusk and watched how people behaved while they were worked to the bone. When the gas lamps flickered on, he lay in the shadows like an oil slick and thought of himself as a piece of the dark, a feature of the city that crept across her rooftops like a ribbon pulled through a bonnet, moving smoothly through the fabric, drawn tight to pull it shut. Elendhaven's very own murderer, Johann of the Night.

For some reason, no one ever remembered his face.

* * *

Elendhaven was Johann's entire world. He was a creature weaned off its oily tit.

Southerners called its harbour the Black Moon of Norden; a fetid crescent that hugged the dark waters of the polar sea. The whole city stank of industry. The air was thick with oil, salt, and smoke, which had long settled into the brick as a slick film, making the streets slippery on even the driest days. It was a foul place: foul scented, foul weathered, and plagued with foul, ugly architecture—squat warehouses peppered with snails and sea grass, mansions carved from heavy, black stone, their thick windows stained green and greasy from exposure to the sea. The tallest points in Elendhaven were the chimneys of the coal refineries. The widest street led south, rutted by the carts that dragged whale offal down from the oil refineries.

Hundreds of years ago, the North Pole had been cut open by searing magic, a horrific event that left the land puckered with craters like the one Elendhaven huddled in. For five centuries, the black waters had been poisoned with an arcane toxin that caused the skin to bubble and the mind to go soggy and loose like bread in broth. Once in a while, the fishermen would pull up an aberration from the ocean floor: something frothing and wet with its insides leaking out its eyes. "Demons and monsters," visitors whispered, "such creatures still sleep inside the Black Moon."

* * *

Johann learned what sort of creature he was by accident.

One day he slipped on a patch of ice. His ankle turned in the wrong direction and plunged him off a roof like a crow with a clipped wing. The ground swallowed him up, and the crunch of his neck against rock reverberated through every joint in his spine. It shuddered through his limbs and popped out the tips of his fingers and toes, a tiny earthquake that made ruin of his bones. He lay absolutely still for ten minutes, and then he stood up and wrenched his skull back into place.

"Well," he said aloud. "That was fucked up."

He began to experiment. Cautiously at first; a pin through the loose skin between thumb and forefinger, a slice just behind the elbow. A dive out a window, a plummet off a tower. His stomach spit out two bullets with elastic ease and he laughed like a boy, giddy and intoxicated. When the watchman took another shot, Johann accepted a round in the clavicle, whooping like a jackal as he jammed a knife into the man's throat. He yanked the bullet out later, painless as a sloop cutting the waves. Johann watched the sun come up, spinning the bloody musket ball between two fingers while whistling a jaunty tune.

He tried to decide later what he was: Johann the Thing. Johann the Demon of Elendhaven. Devil Johann, Johann in Black, Oil-Dark Johann. Monster was the best, his favourite word. The first half was a kiss, the second a hiss. He repeated it to himself again and again: "Monster Johann. *Monster, Monster, Monster.*"

– II –

FLORIAN

Herr Florian Leickenbloom was an old-money dandy. He went out to the shops with a gold-tipped cane tucked under one arm, dressed in burgundy and tarnished gold with a mess of cravat and jewel round his throat. Leickenbloom Manor was the oldest mansion in the city: four floors, twenty-six rooms, and a wrought-iron trim that made it look like an ancient prison that had been garnished by an extremely fussy knitting circle. The Leickenblooms had built Elendhaven, but Florian was the only one left. He lived alone in the manor, undisturbed by visitors or servants. It had been that way for fifteen years.

His profession was accountant, serving wealthy clientele who did not inquire into his personal life. He was a small man with delicate bone structure: high, rouged cheekbones, thin pianist's fingers, cloaked neck-to-wrists-to-ankles to hide the meager width of his rib cage. He moved with the careful gait of someone who'd been fragile since birth.

Johann first saw Florian Leickenbloom at a cheap bar in the industrial district and was drawn to the contrast between the bar's impoverished atmosphere and the gold thread in his coat. Johann slouched behind a lamp with his back against the wall, alert and invisible. Florian was his perfect opposite—a blazing beacon of straw-yellow hair and glass-pale eyes. He nursed his drink for an hour: vodka tonic, blackberry garnish. Johann watched him as he sighed into the glass, turned coins over in his pocket, wound the tips of his pale hair around two fingers. His expensive rings flashed in the lamplight. He was an easy read: the countenance and affected speech of a noble, the lead-lined exhaustion of someone who feels he has suffered beyond the measure of his years. His gestures were stiff, impeccable, *rehearsed,* appropriate for a man of his respectable comportment but undercut in subtle ways, like cracks in fine porcelain. Through those cracks, Johann could see a youthful fear trembling in his clear eyes. An easy read, but by no means an uncomplicated one. Johann thought that he looked rather as if he wanted to be robbed.

So Johann stalked him for three weeks. Elendhaven was a good city for stalking, with its black factories and blade-thin alleyways. It snowed ten and a half months a year and only stopped when the sun came out for a frantic six-week tenure surrounding the summer equinox.

Florian had a very specific routine: he left the house at seven in the morning, fetched a coffee and a jam biscuit from the tea shop nearest his home, arrived by five after eight at the office, where he clacked away at his counting tools and wrote financial reports for the six hours between coffee and business dinner. What only Johann saw was that the windows in his office fogged up when he was inside, that snow turned to steam under his feet. He had observed doors opening with no hands on them and watched Florian's business partners do what he said even when they clearly did not agree with his basic principles. Florian Leickenbloom never paid for his coffee and biscuit in the morning, but the staff at the café did not seem to notice.

Florian Leickenbloom was a sorcerer.

* * *

"I know what you are" was the first thing Johann said to him, his palm braced against the brick and his knife tucked into the hollow of Florian's throat as if it were made to fit there. "And I want what you have."

Florian Leickenbloom's response was to titter at the

back of his throat and nudge—with great and delicate caution—the flat of the blade. He asked, "Is this a robbery, or a murder? If it's the former, could we perhaps make it swift? I've work to do." He seemed to have misunderstood the subtext entirely, and was staring at Johann with an uncommon confidence.

"Neither," Johann said. "I want—"

What *did* he want? Florian's eyes were the colour of light split through a glass of vodka. His wrists were so narrow that they could be snapped with one hand, the bones crushed in a strong palm as easily as the rib cage of a sparrow. But there was a scattering of embers inside his chest that burned as bright as gold trim under a lamp. A ghost nipping at his heels that no one else in all of Elendhaven had noticed. For Johann, the desire to speak to him was instinctual, almost primal. What *did* he want?

"—I want . . . you to hire me. For us to work together. You came into this alley unattended and ended up with a blade against your jugular. Don't you think it's unwise for a man of your stature to go out alone?"

"An unconventional résumé," Florian replied shakily. "But I am afraid I'll have to pass."

"You don't understand, Florian Leickenbloom. I'm not asking you. I'm telling you—I *know* what you are."

Florian's lips went flat. It took him a moment to

respond, and when he did his voice was as brittle as dried seaweed. "How long have you been following me?"

His boldness robbed Johann of his momentum. "Well. I . . ."

"And how is it that you know my name?"

Johann railed: "Oh, that's fucking obvious: your files, your clients. I looked you up in the public archives. I've been—"

"You've been what?"

"*Stalking* you," Johann finished, deflating. "I've been watching you through the windows of your office. I follow you, when you go out." Spoken aloud, it sounded asinine. Hardly the hunt, hardly the actions of a predator. Herr Leickenbloom raised his chin. A thin line of blood appeared beneath the blade and snaked over the metal. Johann watched it trickle all the way to the point of the knife.

"You're not afraid," he observed. "Why aren't you afraid?"

"Oh. Oh no." The air whistled through Florian's teeth as his tone danced along the edge of shrill. "I assure you, I am terrified. You're quite a fearsome man. But I am afraid of most everything, so I've found it useful to evaluate risks with a clear head in the moment and do all my screaming after the fact."

Johann lowered the knife and eased back on his heels. It was not what he had been expecting. It was better, perhaps—this strange man who gave lip while quaking. A branch bending beneath the wind, but not snapping. A grin pulled from one end of his face to the other, slow and pleasant. "Herr Leickenbloom," he said sweetly. "I am about to show you a brilliant trick. I guarantee that you've not seen anything like this before, and unless you take me up on my offer, odds are you'll never see it again."

He took a step back and slit his own throat in a fluid, well-practised movement. The cut flopped open, fish gutted, making his breath stutter and bubble, his vision spin out, showing where all the veins had frayed and turned the blood frothy. He let Herr Leickenbloom get a good look at the carnage before cracking his neck straight with the heel of his palm. The wound healed seamlessly, and Johann drew a gloved finger across his jugular, chuckling at how Florian had grown red and splotchy along his cheekbones. That wasn't all that was red: he'd been sprayed across the face by Johann's blood in a clear, brilliant arc—ear to ear, like a carnival grin. Johann found something about that attractive: his blood marring that immaculate facade. Florian tried to wipe his cheek, but all it did was smear his mouth with crimson.

"Y-you're right," he stuttered. "That is quite the trick."

Johann's vocal cords were still raspy from the slice. "As I was saying, Herr Leickenbloom, I have a business proposition for you."

* * *

Leickenbloom Manor had twenty-six rooms, but Florian only lived in two of them. His bedroom—on the second floor—and an adjacent library with a desk and two chairs. He took all of his meals at restaurants and kept the curtains drawn tight. The common area was as tall and narrow as a chapel, glutted wall to wall with ghostly furniture: wooden chairs, the mantel and cabinets, the dinner table and its companion seats, even the paintings on the wall—all these things smothered in sailcloth, untouched for years. Johann assessed the space from the corner of his vision, with the tips of his fingers. There was dust inches deep gathered beneath the shadow of the fireplace and the cloth was mottled with sunbaked stains. What was the purpose of living like this? he wondered. He wondered if Florian was a man with troubled thoughts; memories that required caging, held still and quiet in the palm of the hand. It reminded Johann, comfortingly, of a morgue.

"The ability of humans to use magic is aberrant," Florian explained, sweeping a tarp off the couch so that

they could sit. It was cherrywood upholstered in chartreuse, frayed at the seams. "Magic is the element the
planet needs to thrive, to produce life, much like the"—
he cast about for an example—"the carbon filament in a
lightbulb. It is the channel of life, the conduit between
nothing and something. But of course, you shouldn't
touch it. You'd be scalded."

"But not you." Johann refused to take a seat. Instead,
he smoothed down the tails of his duster and loomed over
Florian's shoulder.

Florian tipped his head back and looked Johann in the
eyes. Wordlessly, he raised his left arm and began to un-
button his sleeves. He folded the cuff of his jacket to the
elbow, then started on the shirt. Beneath the white fabric his skin was powdery and marred with dark rivers of
bruise. The black wound traced the path of Florian's veins,
his flesh cracking and scabbed around its borders. Johann
whistled and grabbed Florian's arm, running a thumb
over the inside of his wrist. He could feel the texture even
through his glove: coarse and mottled like fresh char-
coal. Florian smiled, thin and tight.

"The difference is that I can survive a few burns."

"So is it an inborn talent?" Johann wondered. "Could
your family always do this shit, or what?"

Florian bent his arm free from Johann's grasp. He was
tense at the question and began fiddling with his rings.

"We . . . n-not for a long time, we haven't. It has been some many years since it was commonplace, is what I mean. I was the first . . . in a while."

Practice of the Old Magic was punishable by death, and for good reason. Magic had nearly destroyed the world. It was over a hundred years since the Mittenwelt had purged the ancient bloodlines of magical aptitude. It survived in the dark corners of the continent, but sorcerers in the modern era were errant throwbacks, mistakes of birth. One had passed through Elendhaven just four years back. Johann had been lucky enough to see the aftermath of his work: a city watchman turned inside out, his guts steaming in the crisp winter air and his bones arranged like a pyre, all stumbled together, clasped skyward like a prayer. Johann had sensed something thrumming in the air that day, like the dissonance that lingers after hitting a piano key. Now that he knew what he was looking for, he could feel the magic filling up the room. Florian stank of it. It jittered out from every nerve in his body. *Not for a long time,* he said. *Aberrant.* Johann heard it properly: Florian Leickenbloom did not think himself a creature made by mortal intent. He was like Johann, one of the Black Moon's monsters.

Johann leant his elbows on the back of the couch. His gaze followed Florian as he stood. "So," he purred. "In that case . . . what's wrong with me, Doc?"

Florian pulled a heavy text from the bookshelf and sneezed, haloed momentarily by a cloud of dust. He dropped the book unceremoniously on the tea table in front of them and let it thump open to a complicated mathematical diagram. The diagram overlaid an image of the globe, but Johann could not make sense of the equations surrounding it.

"Do not call me Doc," Florian said, light toned. "I'm an accountant."

Johann grinned. "Right. So what's the prognosis, *sweetheart*?"

"If I *knew* the 'prognosis,' I would not have brought you to my home." Florian bit his delicate lip, bounced his fingers across the page absentmindedly. "Magic is the energy we create by living and dying. It flows through us on its journey to somewhere else. Someone like me can crack open the cycle and shape that energy into new potential. You—" He sighed. "You're a hiccup, or a flinch. Something that tripped and fell off the carriage, which continues on as if it's forgotten you. You're a living thing that somehow fails to generate or absorb the world's energy."

"Could we avoid framing it in terms of failure?" Johann put his chin in his palm. "It makes me feel so . . . inadequate."

Florian stared at him for a long moment, stroking his

chin thoughtfully. "Johann," he asked quietly, "what is it, exactly, that you want?"

Johann blinked back, expression rictus. Herr Leickenbloom was looking at him with those liquor-pale eyes. *At* him, not through him.

Florian asked again, "What is it that I have that you want?"

"You know what you are," Johann answered: automatically, *instinctually*. "I . . . want to know what I am."

"Your interest is merely philosophical then? Most men, if they woke up and found themselves incapable of dying, would do terrible things with that power."

"Who says I haven't done terrible things with it?"

Florian laughed. "Oh yes, my apologies to the petty cutthroat in a ragged coat. What lofty ambitions! Is that really all you want?"

Johann opened his mouth and found that it was empty. He turned the question over in his head a few times and then said, "Once I climbed the tallest tower I could find. You know, that Geltic Cathedral in the middle of town? I got right up to the top of the steeple and I jumped, just to see what would happen when I hit the ground." He flattened his palm against the arm of the couch and made a squelching noise to demonstrate. "What I found is that I was still hoping for a longer fall."

"I see." Florian steepled his fingers. "That is the best you could think to do with your amazing gift?"

Johann shrugged. "Yeah, well, what the hell would you do with it that's so much better?"

It took Florian a while to respond. He turned his face away from Johann, towards the darkness of the hallway. A slice of orange morning light cut through the gap in the curtains and bisected the shadows of his profile, turned him into obscure shapes against the cracked wallpaper.

He said, "What else but put all the cheques in balance."

– III –

THE SORCERER

They cleared the Leickenbloom kitchen out over the course of an afternoon. They needed the knives, the sink, the polished wooden countertops. Florian did not cook for himself and so those counters were stacked with boxes and junk up to the cupboards.

Florian was quiet the entire time, but Johann kept a careful mental inventory of the items he was handed: three stacks of books with cover illustrations of horses and castles, a musty bin of plaid frocks and skirts (child sized), four boxes with the letters *FLORA* scrawled on them, and a covered painting with a cloth nailed firmly to the frame. That night he slept on a couch two feet too short for his legs. He merrily dangled one ankle over the edge, kicking at the air. He had never slept surrounded by such opulence and it irritated him that Florian was not using it terribly well.

He dreamt about all the things he would do if he

owned a house with twenty-six rooms. He kept friends for longer than a night. He smiled at people he did not intend to stab between the ribs. So many possibilities; he could run a bar, open a hostel, host an orgy every full moon. His most vivid dream was that he hadn't moved from the couch at all. In the dream, Florian covered him with a pale blue sheet and he lay beneath it, muzzled and quiet in the sorcerer's hand until his bones became a part of the house.

They began their experiments with an oyster knife. "Cut," Florian ordered, peering at Johann from over the top of a leather-bound notebook. He was left-handed, Johann noted, and the heel of his palm was already stained with ink early in the morning.

"Cut *where*?"

"Anywhere. Show me what you showed me yesterday."

Johann held the tiny blade up for appraisal. "You want me to slit a throat with this thing? Seriously?"

"No."

"I mean, I could do it. I've done it before. Not to myself, but it's a thing that can be done."

Florian pinched the bridge of his nose. "Cut your arm."

Johann did. It healed cleanly, the skin knitting so

quickly that it almost caught the trailing blade. Florian clutched his book to his chest and watched in naked fascination.

"I don't know what you were expecting," Johann said. "We've been over this already."

Florian looked up at him, eager eyes alight with hunger. "Johann, let me find you a longer fall."

* * *

Florian took him to an abandoned textile factory along the seawall: hollowed out from fire and surrounded by a mile of silence.

"This whole district is dead," Florian tsked, waving his hands. He was dressed in a purple floral print and fur, his tiny hands disappeared into a pair of velvet mittens. "No one manufactures clothes out of Elendhaven anymore, not even to evade the new child labour laws down past Sandherst."

The factory was built into a cradle of stone, as if the cliff were a great hand holding it in place. Johann teetered over the edge of the roof and watched the waves smash against the black rock. The sea battered the cliff like a rabid animal, frothing salt spittle around dark stone teeth. It was going to split him open, chew him up. It was going to devastate his body so completely that it probably wouldn't even hurt until he was almost healed. His mouth was watering, and he licked his lips in anticipation.

"Well?" Florian sounded impatient. Johann looked him over, all pale and shivering inside his winter frock. He was tapping his foot off-time with his breathing. "Are you going to jump?" he asked. "Or shall I have to push you?"

Johann spent the afternoon throwing himself into the ocean, dashing himself against the rocks like a shipwreck. Florian huddled on the shore and took notes. Johann tried to imagine what they said as a way to amuse himself on the long climb back up the service ladder. *First Trial. Left arm only broken in three places, disappointing. Second Trial. Skull fractures heal faster and more efficiently than a cracked thighbone. Fascinating. I have seen the inside of Johann's stomach. His guts are the colour of rhubarb custard.*

When he finally asked, Florian gave his pen a studious flourish and smiled with a measure of sincerity. "Equations," he said. "Measurements: distance of the fall, the rate of your regeneration."

Johann didn't much care for equations. Mathematics was an area of study that he had never succeeded in teaching himself. "That's some ripe tedium," he muttered, and plopped himself down to look over Florian's shoulder. "What does that accomplish?"

He felt Florian bristle beneath his chin. "I'm a student of economics," he explained, tone defensive. "Tracking patterns and behaviour through comparative equations. I am taking the mathematical shape of you."

"Yeah, well, if that's all you wanted, you just had to ask, *honeydew*. You don't need to add three plus six to get me out of my clothes."

Florian hummed and ignored him in favour of his sums. As revenge, Johann shook himself dry like a dog, spraying Florian and his notes with specks of foamy seawater. Florian shrieked and leapt to his feet. "You—" His finger shook where he angled it at Johann in accusatory offense. "Y-you!"

"Me?" Johann snickered, barely able to contain himself.

What Johann learned about Florian Leickenbloom didn't need an equation. It took just this—a few well-placed words, a lack of tact—to discover that he lost his breath when he giggled, covering his mouth politely like the girls from the convent school. Johann jounced to his feet and offered Florian a hand.

"You're awful," Florian hissed out between chuckles. "You're a vile creature."

"Herr Leickenbloom, *please*." Johann smiled easily.

"Don't underestimate me. I'm more than vile; I'm an honest-to-god *monster*."

* * *

Florian did not forget Johann's business proposition. "If it's unwise for me to go out alone," he said, with a shrewd, feline smile, "I suppose that from now on I shall have to take you with me." He trussed Johann up in cobalt and silver and brought him about on his daily chores.

If Johann was, as he liked to think of himself, the monster of Elendhaven's night, Florian was the monster of its mornings and afternoons. Everyone knew Florian's face and name. The factory owners tripped over themselves in the streets to greet him. Herr Leickenbloom, they called him, perfectly formal, precisely deferential.

The day after the cliff they met with the Sudengelt Ambassador and three companions outside the bakery. The Ambassador bowed and kissed Florian's family ring.

"Herr Leickenbloom, gutenmorn," he huffed, breath misting between his plump lips. He ceased genuflecting and slipped a deft hand around the hip of the woman accompanying him. "Might I introduce you to my ward, Eleanor? It's her first trip north."

Florian flushed politely and took Eleanor's hand. "Gutenmorn, madame," he said shyly. She bowed, hiding her face behind a curtain of black curls.

"Eleanor, if you've been told there are no proper gentlemen in Elendhaven, your informant has never met Florian Leickenbloom." The man who spoke was lean and freckled, with carrot-red hair, a shade not often seen in the northern states. He was chewing on a black cigar beneath the curtain of his moustache.

"There is no need to puff me up in front of company, Ansley," Florian demurred. "I'm sure Eleanor has been treated with hospitality as lovely as our weather."

The third man—blond, long nosed, and dressed ostentatiously in white—chuckled. Eleanor's dark eyes went wide and she looked quite earnest when she said, "The weather *is* lovely. I've never seen such remarkable skies."

Florian released her hand. "The North paints the sunrise in colours undreamt in Mittengelt and Sudengelt."

"Truly. I could, however, do with a touch more daylight."

"Then you must visit us in the summer, Lady Eleanor. At the equinox, the sun hardly sets for longer than it takes to prepare a pot of tea."

"Ah yes, I'd heard so. . . ." Eleanor adjusted one of her gloves and shivered. "But the winters . . ."

"Are long and dark," Florian affirmed. "But it is those long nights that make a northern summer so sweet."

"Florian is a true native of the Black Moon," the Ambassador explained. "His family has been here since the founding of Elendhaven."

"Yes," Ansley mused, stroking his beard. "You might even call Herr Leickenbloom a local fixture. One of our very finest landmarks."

Neither Ansley, nor the Ambassador, nor Eleanor, nor the long-nosed man in white took notice of Johann, so he—skulking behind Florian like his sharp-toothed, long-boned shadow—focused on the shape and slant of Florian's shoulders. On the way he held himself when speaking courteously. It was a submissive silhouette, the same prey-animal contour that had tricked Johann when they first met. Florian flowed in and out of it effortlessly, a physical architecture far more elaborate than Johann's own.

"His ward," Ansley sneered when the Ambassador led Eleanor away. "What a way to describe a kept woman."

Florian—where no one but Johann could see—displayed a subtle disgust: one nostril flared, and a cheek sucked in where he was biting it shut. Herr Long-Nose added, in a melodic accent, "You'd think he'd have the decency to share since you're putting them up."

"Ansley," Florian cut in, tone clipped and amiable.

"What has you meeting with foreigners so early in the day?"

Ansley tapped ash from his cigar. He was a broad man, not as tall as Johann, but he dwarfed Florian, who might have been mistaken for a woman from behind. "Have you met Herr Charpentier?" Long-Nose tipped his hat. "He's looking to expand the railroads."

"Yes." Charpentier took Florian's offered hand and shook it. "Elendhaven still uses a narrow gauge. We would have the rails broadened so that freight wagons may come and go."

"You will not be the first one who's tried that," Florian said.

"Ah—but I will be the *last,* monsieur. You can be sure of that." Charpentier's eyes glittered when he laughed.

Florian did not laugh back. He clasped Charpentier's hand tight.

"Are you certain? Elendhaven is built on ancient rock so solid that trees cannot find root. Digging through rock is slow work, wet and cold. We are prone to industrial accidents. One week here beneath the shroud of winter and you will reconsider."

Something dark passed over Charpentier's face. In Florian's expression, Johann saw a scattering of embers. A ghost of a smile. A man who knew exactly what he was—

—and then Ansley slapped him on the back. Florian's response was to buck forward two steps and start coughing. Charpentier tugged his hand free. Looking a little lost, he rubbed it where Florian had touched him.

"Don't mind Florian, Herr Charpentier," Ansley crowed. "He's an incurable pessimist. But if there's one thing he enjoys, it's an elegantly balanced budget. Once we have him run the numbers, you'll earn his support."

"Oh, doubtlessly," Florian replied, still fluttering away beneath his veil of false fragility. Johann watched him wave the men off, expression placid and pleasant until they turned the corner. "You see that?" he scoffed once he and Johann were alone. "I am nearly thirty years old and they treat me as if I am still a child. A fragile bauble."

"Aren't you?" Johann sidled up to him and tapped him on the head. Florian hardly came up to his shoulders.

"I am as he said." Florian tucked his hands into the folds of his elbows. "An Elendhaven landmark. A public spectacle of mourning. My childhood tragedy has turned me glacial in the eyes of others. I am trapped in ice, a curiosity in a glass jar."

Johann folded the words cautiously and tucked them away. *Tragedy, glass jars.* Wouldn't do well to push too hard too soon, or he might shatter.

They strolled through the city square, passing beneath the statue of Hallandrette, God-Queen of the northern ocean. She was wreathed in seaweed and bar-nacles, her skeletal hands held aloft as if she were claw-ing her way towards the surface. Johann didn't know any of the stories behind the statue, but he always found it strange that the Queen of the Sea should be carved to look as if she were drowning.

Florian dug in his pocket and flicked a gold coin into her fountain. It was sucked beneath the oily surface and lost forever to the dark water. "Ansley means to re-open the silver mines," he muttered. To himself, but Johann leapt to fill the gap anyway.

"Why's that a bad thing?"

Florian sighed. "Ansley's parents were Sandherst born. He thinks himself a man of Elendhaven, but he knows nothing about us."

It was not an answer to Johann's question, but it was all he offered. *Good enough for now,* Johann thought. He sat himself on the edge of the fountain and grabbed Flo-rian by the fingers.

"Hey. Sit down for a minute," he said, patting the space beside him. With an hour until noon, the park sur-rounding Hallandrette's fountain was empty.

"I am not sitting on those stones," Florian groused. "This coat cost three hundred marks."

"You *are* a delicate bauble." Johann snickered. He

paused artfully before adding, "A delicate bauble capable of fucking around with a man's head."

Florian choked on his next breath. "*E-excuse* me?" he stuttered, his face caught halfway between indignant and horrified, as if he thought Johann were making a pass at him.

"You control people," said Johann, conversationally. "With your sorcery, right? Get your creepy little fingers all inside their heads?"

Florian's vision flitted around the court nervously and he looked for a moment as if he might lie. Instead, he took a deep breath and brushed the light dusting of snow from his shoulders. "Yes," he said, but did not elaborate.

"Can you do it to anyone?"

"Well, I've not tried it on every individual in Elendhaven, Johann, so I could not give you a comprehensive answer."

"But most people, right?"

Florian hesitated, looked away. ". . . Yes."

"You did it to the guy with the weird nose?"

"The slightest tweak." Florian flipped his hair. "The mildest of cloudings."

"Okay, so why don't you do it to"—Johann swirled one of his fingers about in the air—"the Ambassador's lady friend, hmm? Make her *your* lady friend, for a night?"

Florian's vision snapped up. "*Absolutely* not."

"*Why* not?"

He shook his head. "I . . . I *do not* use magic carelessly, or as a jest. Especially not magic as dangerous as—"

Johann kicked out a leg to bump Florian lightly in the shin. "You only use it to, what, smooth over rocky business relations?"

"That is completely different."

"Or so that you don't have to pay for coffee?"

"You!" Florian's cheeks puffed out in an expression of charming indignation, but they deflated before he could get properly shrill. Instead, he rubbed the center of his forehead and swayed on his feet, making muffled noises at the back of his throat that might have been grunting or laughter. "Oh, Johann. You did quite a job of stalking me, but you haven't the faintest idea what I'm about, do you?"

Johann liked this look on Florian: playful and cruel. He eased back on his palms and gazed at him. "So tell me about it."

Florian bent forward, hands on his knees. "This coat," he whispered, "cost three hundred marks. How could a man of my circumstances afford such a thing?"

"You're old money, Leickenbloom. Is this a trick question?"

Florian tapped Johann's nose. "The Old Houses have

been broke for centuries, their money dispersed into land or robbed by the trading companies. The nobles in Mittengelt and the southern colonies rot in their perfumed manors, too proud to beg for charity, but in the North they simply died. I am the last Leickenbloom. The coffers were empty before my mother's grandfather was even conceived."

"What's your point?"

"Ansley—that man's parents leveraged the debt from my father's factory. That was the first brick laid in their fortune. Were I not so good at what I do, it would have become the keystone. He could have owned me, and the better part of Elendhaven as well. Instead, he wants to re-open the silver mines. Look around you, Johann." Florian swept his arm across the skyline. "This city is drowning. All Elendhaven was ever meant to be was a factory the length and breadth of a city, and now it cannot even do that. The fur trade, fisheries, textiles, and lumber . . . even the oil refinery is suffocating."

"I know, I know," Johann said. "Spare the lecture, sweetheart. Even a gutter-shit like me reads the papers."

Florian's smile made the shape of a boy telling a precious secret joke for the first time ever. He put his mouth next to Johann's ear and whispered, "What would you say if I told you that I was the architect of all of this?"

"*All* of it?" Johann echoed, skeptical.

"Yes, ye— Well, *no,* I didn't *cause* the failure, if we're going to be pedantic—"

"Of course, you just fucking *hate* being pedantic."

Florian flicked Johann between the eyes. "You asked the question, Johann; do me the favour of listening to at least part of the explanation."

Johann rubbed the sore spot and gazed up at Florian, his eyes hooded beneath his bangs: alert, fascinated, and fond. "Okay, Herr Leickenbloom. How does one *boy*—a bauble in a glass jar—destroy the economy of an entire city?"

"It's easy enough to keep a wound bleeding once it's been made. So I"—Florian tapped one of his temples, his body language mischievous but his voice trembling at the border of fury—"put my *creepy* fingers into the robber barons' heads, and I convince them to use their *own* fingers to peel off the scab before it forms. It's subtle work, but for the past six years these industry men and conceited governors have come to rely on me, and I point them in the wrong direction every time. That is what I use my magic for: funnelling their money into my own pocket and never spending a lick of it on their foul coffee and cake." He spit the last words onto the ground between them.

Johann looked at him for a long time. Florian was the colour and temper of a white flame, his skin and hair porcelain bright against the coal-stained edifices and the dark grey sky. Slowly and with great deliberation, Johann stood up. He towered over Florian and asked in a low voice, "Cinnamon-sugar, duckling-sweet, my little *honey-flower* . . . what is it, exactly, that you want?"

Florian craned back his neck and smiled serenely. He held out his hand and asked, "May I have a knife?"

Johann handed him his favourite boning knife. He didn't move as Florian lifted one of his hands and began to peel away the glove.

He sliced Johann's hand along the path of his Heart line. He cut so deep that the blade drew up the dark blood, the deep blood. "Johann, you might not believe it, but I am a philanthropist"—he laughed to himself—"and I am going to bleed you for the same reason that I have bled Elendhaven."

"And why is that?"

Florian dipped his forefinger into the pool of blood in Johann's palm and licked it, smiling with bloodstained teeth. "This city has some very hefty debts to settle."

*   *   *

That night, Johann passed by the shrouded portrait on his way down from the study. He stopped in front of it and flexed his fingers.

The sheet came away easily. The fabric was old and fragile from moths and the long winter's humidity. The painting beneath was of Florian as a child. He was perhaps eight years old and already possessed of a profound misery. Beside him was a young girl in a plaid frock. Her posture was the opposite of Florian's dreary, practised elegance: there was defiance in her sloppy slouch and a quirk to her lip that suggested she had been bribed a great deal to sit still. Otherwise, she was Florian's perfect mirror.

"Oh," Johann said out loud. "Well, isn't *that* interesting."

– IV –

THE THING WITH
NO NAME

When Johann was still an unnamed thing he came across a corpse that gave him pause. It was caught by the fold of skin above its hip on a serrated outcropping of rock, leaking a thread of bile the colour and texture of breakfast custard into the tide that spit it up. The body was bloated and milky from a week's exposure to the ocean, but the waxy sheen of fat coating the skin did not hide the damage it had suffered before passing. Beneath the skin there were blackened colonies of tumorous growth: on either side of the neck, beneath the arms, up the insides of the thighs, cushioning its curdled genitals. Some of the growths had popped like seed bulbs, making crags and ruin of the corpse's skin. The thing knelt beside it for minutes, maybe hours—it had been difficult to tell the difference between the two before he had a name—and tried to imagine the circumstances that had caused its body to stop working.

The nameless child was familiar with slit throats and

cracked skulls—the things that humans could do to one another, the counterbalance of violence and power—but the weight of disease was inconceivable. A body betraying itself.

At the time, Florian—only twelve years old—was sat among corpses, sewing a stone into the lining of his mother's favourite coat. A week earlier he'd hoped for nothing more dearly than to be the next one struck dead.

"Would you like to see what I've been working on?" Florian asked Johann, fifteen years later.

"More facts and sums? I need something tastier to whet my appetite, Herr Leickenbloom."

"Oh, don't worry about that." Florian tapped him on the wrist comfortingly. "You'll like this. You've done your tricks, Johann. Now let me perform mine."

* * *

For his tricks, Florian required materials.

"Bring me *something*. Preferably alive."

Some "thing." Florian had emphasized the second half of the word with a punctuated press of the tongue to the teeth. Not a person, then. Most of the animals native to the Norden craters were long extinct for the usual reasons: arcane corruption, pollution, the invention of the musket. Some, however, survived. Deer-legged wolves haunted the borders of the city and often lined the space between skin and ribs with man flesh during particularly nasty winters. Johann had empathy for the wolves so he decided to fetch Florian a seal, for which he held no regard. The waters surrounding the city were overfished recently, but the seals were as fat as ever. Probably they feasted on whatever seabed feature made the water bubble and stink in the springtime. There was a metaphor in that, Johann thought, about a city consuming itself, Florian knocking back coins like a shot of whiskey, the ink from his equations bleeding into the soil, what there was of it. If only Florian were the type of man who appreciated poetry, Johann could have flattered him to blushing.

Johann had no idea how to fish, and he spent an awful hour thrashing about the shore tossing knives at fat shadows and getting sand down the backs of his boots. He at last bought a net for two and a half marks and sat on the dock eating a loaf of salted beef haunch. The tide came in so deep that he was soaked up to the knees and he got the tails of Florian's lovely gift-coat crusted in salt.

At high moon, a drunken sailor wandered by and began jostling him. "Ah, what's this now? That coat must be worth more than my wife! A dandy fancies himself a fisherman?"

Johann didn't like sailors much, so when the drunkard attempted to correct the spread of his net he tipped the man into the harbour and set his foot on his back until he stopped struggling. He hummed and licked meat salt off the fingers of his gloves before remembering the cadence of Florian's voice as he'd said, *And please, try not to make me an accessory to murder.*

Magnanimously, he flipped the sailor over with the toe of his boot and let him dead-float towards the shore. A fifty-fifty chance, he told himself, that he'd wake up before the water settled in his lungs.

When he finally took a seal home to Herr Leickenbloom, Florian crinkled his nose in disgust and muttered, "I said *alive,* preferably."

Still, he had Johann slice the animal open.

"So magic can bring the dead back to life?" Johann asked, watching Florian press a hand to the seal's lung and fill it with air.

"Not true life," Florian said. "You can make the respiratory system react, pump the ventricles. But there is nothing going on inside."

Johann hitched himself up on Florian's worktable and grinned. "So like me then?"

"Well." Florian sniffed. "You are a creature of base instincts. I suppose I could believe it. Would you hand me the syringe, please?"

If only Florian knew *how* base. Johann's gloved fingers brushed against Florian's as he handed him the brass needle.

"The plague that swept through Elendhaven fifteen years ago was the result of a pernicious germ, carried on the backs of southern sparrows. The Mittengelt transplants were so certain it was a local illness that their methods for combating it were entirely ineffective."

"And you're all steamed up about that, so now you're trying to re-create it?"

Florian glowered at him from beneath the wisps of his bangs. "Would you let me finish?"

"Sorry, darling, I'm just trying to grease the machinery of the conversation."

"I am not *trying* to re-create it. I've already done so. I've been incubating a strain for some time, but even with magic it's difficult to replicate the effect I am aiming for."

"And what effect is that?"

Florian smiled—bright and blade sharp—and said, "Let me show you."

He splayed and tip-tapped his fingers across the breadth of the carcass like it was a piano. Where the pads of his fingers touched, the flesh bubbled and bulged into horrible shapes, as if Florian were sewing rocks beneath the surface of the membrane. He had his sleeves rolled up to the elbows so that Johann could watch the magic

flow through his blood. His veins emitted a faint light between the scab-crust of their wounding, and the light
made his arms unnervingly translucent. His skin looked
like the flesh of an insect beneath the exoskeleton; the
arcane bioluminescence highlighted the dark sleepless
ditches under his eyes, making him hollow, unnatural, in-
substantial. Johann had to clutch a hand to his throat to
keep the flash of affection that rocked through him caged
in his esophagus where it belonged. Oh, Florian was a
pretty little thing. Too pretty, too aware of the length of
his eyelashes and the feminine tilt of his jawline. No one
would expect that boyish half smile, that nervous wring-
ing of the wrist, to conceal a monster.

Monster, Monster, Monster, Johann said to himself, *the
first half a kiss, the second a hiss.*

* * *

The shoreline down beneath the black cliffs was the
warmest place in Elendhaven. There was a narrow stretch
of grey and blue sand between the cliffs and the water,
speckled with rocks and shells and the soft residue of
jellyfish. This was where Johann and Florian went walking on a church-day morning.

The wind whipped their jackets around their knees
and the salt in the air raked their cheeks raw, but this far

beneath the tidemark the humidity sucked the frost from the air. Florian knelt at the water's edge and scooped up a handful of frigid water between his palms. It was the colour of coal.

"You've never been outside Elendhaven, have you?" Florian asked. Johann shook his head. Florian let the water flow from the gaps between his fingers. "Then you don't know this, but everywhere else in the world, water is clear. If you pour it into a glass, you can see straight through it."

Johann couldn't picture it. He helped Florian to his feet. "So, what? You wanna see what's at the bottom of the ocean?"

The edges of Florian's mouth piqued unevenly. He shook out of Johann's grasp and resumed walking.

"Do you know what a hallankind is?"

"Sure." Johann kicked at a speckled red shell that peered out through the sand. It crumbled to dust under his boot. "It's dock slang for lad-whores. For little boy prostitutes."

"An ancient term transformed into crude modern vernacular. Here." Florian dipped gingerly, right at the sodden border cut by the tide, and plucked out a stone: perfectly round, an inch in diameter and opalescent in sheen. He held it aloft for Johann's benefit. "The oldest stories of the North called these rocks Hallandrette's Roe.

She lays her clutch along the beach, and protects them from the destructive hands of mortal beings." Florian turned on his heel and pitched the stone at the cliff-wall as hard as he could. It bounced off the slate harmlessly. "See? Hard stone. Unbreakable."

Johann frowned. "How do you crack one open, then?"

Florian smiled, secretive. "A privilege reserved for Hallandrette's chosen. When a wretched child, one wronged or wounded deep in the soul, throws what they love most in the ocean they may cast a roe against the stone and a hallankind will be born. Keep the stone in their pocket and the Queen sends to them one of her children."

"A friend for the lonely soul."

"A companion," Florian affirmed, "made from the same dark matter that coats the bottom of the Nord Sea. A hallankind will love that wretched child as a brother or sister. They will drag whoever wronged their brother-sister-friend into the sea and wring them through the spines of their mother's baleen until they are foam and sea particle, forgotten in the cradle of her belly."

Florian was breathing heavily from the effort of his speech. His eyes were wet and lucid, fixed on some distant point beyond the horizon. He trembled, unnoticed, in the chill. Johann reached out to brush a lock of hair from his face and Florian met his eyes, sudden and fierce.

"Your eyes are black as the sea," Florian told him. The words were almost an accusation. Johann breathed a few cautious beats before responding.

"That's sweet, peach. You're saying that I was made for you?"

Florian let out a snort. "Of course not. My hallankind never hatched, and she would hardly have been a thing like *you*. No, Johann . . . you belonged to someone far more wretched than I. More deserving of Hallandrette's pity."

"More wretched is right. Poor bastard never got the chance to use me."

"Don't be ridiculous," Florian snapped, suddenly serious. "It's a story, Johann, a myth. But I will be needing the stones. They contain traces of an extremely rare metal. Sixteen should be enough."

Johann clicked his tongue in quiet irritation. "Whatever you say, Boss." He lifted the edge of his jacket to make a sling for the stones. After a moment, he added, "But nevertheless, you know, here I am."

"I know." Florian dropped a polished roe into Johann's coat. "What a perfect and unexpected gift for the child that never grew old." He rapped a finger against Johann's chest. "A toy that cannot be broken."

ELENDHAVEN

I t's not so bad," said Ansley, of the railroad.

And certainly, it ran just fine from the outskirts of town down the eastern coast. The problem was the length stretching from the city center to the base of the mountain. Fifteen years of disuse saw the track weather warped and salt eaten. The wooden slats stank of rot, and the space between them was coated in snails and barnacles.

"The problem," Florian mulled, standing on his tiptoes so that he could gesture over the edge of the cliff, "is that seawater washes over the track if it storms during high tide. I remember once, when I was a child, a freight derailed and took the locomotive with it out to sea. The driver escaped, but they lost six men trying to drag the payload back to shore."

"A wider gauge means a steadier train," said the Ambassador, adjusting the lapels of his cotton suit. He was wearing a peculiar shade of green—yellow tinged and gold lined. On a sunny day it would have shimmered with layered dimensions like a pearl. Beneath Elendhaven's grey skies it was the colour of puke.

"Even better, monsieur." Herr Charpentier slung an arm around Florian's shoulders. "We could blast a path through the mountain."

Johann stood with his toes lined up to the edge of the cliff. He tossed a look over his shoulder to catch Florian bristling under Charpentier's advance like a hermit crab skittering back into its shell. Florian often leapt away from casual touch like he was coming into contact with hot iron. Johann tugged at the tip of his glove with his teeth—didn't pull it off the whole way, but savoured the sensation of the leather rolling over the thick artery in his wrist. Johann didn't like to leave fingerprints, or to touch things that were alive, or to be touched back. Still, he wondered what Florian's skin felt like once the greasepaint was smudged off.

"Johann," Florian called him to attention. His "boss" was standing with crossed arms and raised hackles, puffed up and exasperated and trying very hard to look grown-up. Oh, his theatre of civility was well practised, but Johann could see the cracks, so deep they were the colour of the ocean.

"Sorry, Boss." Johann shoved his hands in his pockets and strolled towards the track. "Got distracted by the view."

Herr Charpentier was dangling a set of metal calipers from one palm. "Before I make any decisions, I need to know how the iron has bent."

Johann took the calipers, turned them about in his hand. He shot Florian a puzzled look: *What am I supposed to do with these?* Florian's smile showed teeth. *Play along.*

So Johann tried to look busy, making studious gestures, exaggerated pretensions at being a capable manservant. He knelt in the sludge and pried the calipers open. They looked like a pair of legs, spread-eagle. Johann eased them apart salaciously, stroking his thumb down the long curve of the upper thigh. Florian caught his little jest—Johann made sure of it. When he winked, a flash of lucid pique lit Florian's face up like a bolt of lightning. It lasted about that long, too. Florian took a wide step across the track so that he could—*subtly*—kick Johann with the heel of his boot as he passed.

"I-is it really possible to cut through a mountain?" he asked Charpentier, masking his vexation beneath breathy wonder. "These cliffs are a th-thousand . . . a thousand *thousand* years old. It's thought that the harbour was once a massive, primeval volcano that spewed so much smoke from just one blast that it could shadow the entire earth. That's how this mountain was formed—from an eon of unbroken eruption."

"Herr Leickenbloom, I hope you don't mind me saying, but you are terribly provincial. With modern explosives, anything is possible," Charpentier chirped, unconcerned for and uninterested in Florian's natural-history lecture. "If one can build a mine, surely one can shear the mountain in half."

"Besides, the slate is brittle." Ansley bent down to snatch a rock off the ground. He snapped it in half between thumb and forefinger, then crumbled it to dust in his palm. "Or are you that concerned for the conservation of our history, Florian?"

Florian fiddled with the tips of his hair and gazed at the mountain. "It *is* rather lovely in its own way, don't you think?"

Johann, scraping the calipers against the iron, followed the tilt of Florian's chin with his eyes. He'd never given much thought to the mountain. It was pale at the bottom and dark at the top, flat headed and jagged where it met the sea, cut through with bands of black and silver, blue ribbons of silt that glimmered in the starlight. Maybe it *was* unique; Johann had no way of knowing what else a mountain should look like.

"You can see the passage of time in the layers of sediment. The rigours and transformations of the land, the strength of the sea, the suffering and joy of the people who've lived here."

"But it casts a dark shadow over the city, does it not?"

the Ambassador muttered, pulling a handkerchief from his front pocket. "You know, I only live here three months of the year, but the feeling the city gives me . . . Elendhaven drags behind me like I've got shackles on both ankles. Silver is a bright metal, hearty too. It's an ideal conductor and does not corrode easily. Polish it and it can be used as a mirror. I think that this city needs a little silver, and far less shadow. Ansley's proposal would be like pulling the curtains open on a clear morning—it would shine light into the dark corners."

Florian quirked an eyebrow. "And what do you expect to find in those dark corners?"

"Well—" The Ambassador paused to blow his nose. Upon closer examination, it was clear that his eyes were red ringed and watery; his hands trembled where they clutched the patterned hemline of his napkin. "You've heard what they say, Herr Leickenbloom: monsters still sleep beneath the Black Moon."

"It's inside," Florian whispered.

"Hmm?"

"Monsters still sleep inside the Black Moon," he said, touching a knuckle to his chin. "Not beneath. You had the saying rather confused."

The words lingered in the air like fog. Johann smiled to himself as he used the calipers to lever a railroad spike free from its mooring.

Finally, the Ambassador let out a deflated chuckle. He clapped a friendly hand on Florian's shoulder and said, "The distinction is rather immaterial, is it not?"

The Ambassador excused himself, Ansley and Herr Charpentier tracking his footsteps. Florian stared after the men for a very long time, a quizzical expression tugging at his mouth.

Johann pulled himself to his feet. "Herr Charpentier forgot his little metal nether parts," he said, tossing the calipers over his shoulder and pocketing the rail spike. He liked the weight of it in his coat.

"He forgot about *you*," Florian corrected. "That was strange, don't you think?"

"What was strange about it?"

Florian didn't answer, or pay Johann any mind. That was an unacceptable state of affairs, so Johann leant an elbow on the crown of Florian's head. His hair was so light and fine that it required only a bit of mussing to fluff up like a dandelion.

Florian ducked out from under Johann's arm, batting at him with a mittened hand. "Never mind," he said testily. "We still have work to do."

Johann spared one last look towards the ocean, pulled all the way out for low tide so that the entire ragged gash of the shore could be seen. Calm now, a parent with a steady hand who punished only those children who turned their cheek. Whether he understood it or not, Florian had spoken the elemental truth of Elendhaven—the harbour was a womb, not a shroud.

* * *

"The problem is that I've been stumbling about in the dark."

Florian was entertaining Johann in his study. "Entertaining" was the formal term for rich dilettantes letting other rich dilettantes get drunk in their mansions, potentially for several days straight. Johann had slunk himself into a party like that once: a masked soiree on the edge of town, a sitting room stuffed to the brim with foreign fabrics and hashish. He wondered if that had been Ansley's affair, or an affair hosted by one of Ansley's associates. He couldn't remember seeing Ansley there, but it occurred to him now that he often looked through people the same way they looked through him. He knew the bricks in Elendhaven's most dilapidated streets better than he knew the faces of the grey crowds who trudged through them. For instance, there was a crack that ran from the town square to the gutter behind the whale-oil refinery. It was the width of a thumb, two fingers deep. It took ten minutes to walk the length of that crack leisurely, and in spring it filled up with purple weeds and the bloated carcasses of slugs. Once, Johann had gutted a curious barman at the mouth of the street and followed the blood down the crack until it sank into the ground.

Johann had been sleeping in Leickenbloom Manor for two weeks and Florian had not once offered him pipe or drink. What *entertained* him was watching Florian hitch himself up on tiptoes to reach the top shelf of his personal library. The motion pulled the cinched fabric at his waist tight, emphasized his ankles. He swayed beneath the weight of the book he retrieved from the shelf, doing a clumsy little dance across the room before setting it on his desk with a heavy thud.

"The foundational myths of our culture suggest that magic can do anything," Florian said, rapping his fingers along the front of the book. It was wood cased, bound with copper twine and yellowed from age. No inscription. "The great Wizard Barons could control a man from miles away with just a drop of his blood."

"But not you?"

"No. Not me. It's a talent that has to be taught, *practised,* and my family burned almost all our old texts."

"What *can* you do?"

"I can"—he chewed his lip in dissatisfaction—"make a suggestion that will most certainly be followed. I can work magic into things that already exist. But *carefully.* Whenever I use my power I can feel . . . a great abyss yawning open beneath me. It's the same feeling I get standing at the edge of the ocean: staring into another world that I can touch but would surely drown in were I to wade out too far."

"Your parents never taught you how to swim?"

"My parents didn't teach me much of anything." Florian opened the book, licked his thumb to pry the pages open. Apropos of nothing, he asked, "Did you know that silver is used by Mage Hunters?"

"Mmm-hmm, what for?" Johann was only halfway listening. Florian loved to ramble about arcane materials and obscure theories and his family history, as if he'd never known a person with whom he could hold a conversation about anything unrelated to sums and equations and the weather. *That* was not an obscure theory: Johann had plenty evidence to think it true.

"If I *knew* what for, I'd have no reason to worry."

"*Are* you worried?" Johann asked, swinging out of his seat so that he could loom over the desk at Florian's side. "You think that Ansley has cottoned on to the fact that you're a wizard? Think he wants to drown the city in silver to flush you out?"

Florian brushed a lock of hair out of his face and smirked. "Nothing that drastic. Besides, Ansley has plenty of silver of his own. The last thing my grandmother did before she died was pawn all our heirlooms to the landed gentry. I'm sure most of the silver ended up in his parents' cellar."

"You know, Florian, you hold an awful lot of grudges for such a tiny, tiny man."

"Oh, Johann." Florian tittered. "A *grudge* would suggest that my grievances were unwarranted. But I'm not petty. The scales on which I weigh justice would not be nudged by something so small and petty as a dinnerware set. I . . . ," He trailed off. His hair fell back in his face.

"You what?" Johann murmured, tucking the lock back behind Florian's ear where it belonged.

Florian's tone was as lost as his gaze. "Don't you feel it, sometimes? As if the world wants to consume itself?" He shook his head. "Cleaving through a mountain that's stood since the days of the Allfather. What's the point of thinking such a thing?"

"That big-nosed nobleman was right—you *are* provincial, Herr Leickenbloom."

Florian whapped him on the chest. "You—you've done nothing today but needle me and ask asinine questions."

"I thought you enjoyed being given a chance to monologue, sweetling." Johann poked the tip of his nose in retaliation, and savoured how stupid and childish it looked when wrinkled.

"If you're going to be like that, then at least ask me better questions."

"Fine. Where, specifically, do I fit into all of this? What do I owe you for my room and board?"

"Ah, that." Florian hooked his thumbs beneath Johann's lapels and began crawling one hand up his chest. Not sensually: he was counting Johann's ribs. "You must have a guess or two. What's the one thing you're good for?"

Johann thought about that for a moment. Then he peeled off a glove—slowly, watching the way Florian watched him with bright, hungry eyes. Not hungry for his flesh, but for what pulsed beneath it. Johann bit into his thumb until it bled. Florian's eyes tracked the blood as it beaded against the hard edge of Johann's cuticle before dripping onto the open book.

"You want your plague to . . . be un-killable," he said, pressing his wound shut. Spoken aloud, it was obvious.

"Old Magic is transference," Florian said softly. He smeared the blood down the center of the page. The paper drank it up. "Not addition. Not alteration. *That's* the knowledge we lost when my family burned the old library. If I could figure out how to transfer your essence . . . well . . ."

Something about the plan scratched at the back of Johann's head. Florian's personality was fastidious, almost compulsive. It seemed odd for him to make a plan with such ambiguous parameters. "That's a little open-ended, don't you think? What happens after that?"

Florian huffed. "If you *really* want to know what it is I need you for, it's this." He produced a list from one of his pockets, waved it in Johann's face. "I've been in dire need of a servant to fetch my groceries for years."

* * *

Florian's grocery list included: a fleam for bloodletting, a brass-screw tourniquet, a bottle of formaldehyde, forceps, an assortment of glass vials with their cork stoppers intact, one tenaculum—which Florian had to draw Johann an instructive picture of—and a bag of candied dates from the general store.

Elendhaven's hospital was a featureless redbrick building three storeys high. Johann entered through the morgue, using the same waste chute he'd used as an exit the few times he'd accidentally ended up the coroner's guest. The fleam and the fluid were easy enough to nick from the morgue cabinet. For the rest of it, he had to slip into the second-floor surgery suite. It was early morning and the chilly halls were dark and empty. There was one doctor present, sitting in an open-door office tapping away at his counting machine, dipping his thumb under his spectacles to dig the mucus out of his tear ducts. Johann slipped past him between clicks of the abacus, twirling his recently acquired forceps around one finger. On his way back to the morgue, he heard a familiar voice drifting up the staircase.

". . . teas . . . ey've not done anyth . . . orestall the fever."

Johann stopped in his tracks—forceps jolting to a stop against his wrist—and listened.

". . . umping to conclusions, Herr Ambassador."

"I'm certain of it. The fever is arcane in nature. The last two aides I brought north with me have succumbed to it."

Johann slid up flat against the wall to listen. The Ambassador's voice was wet, like the noise a drain makes when clogged with gristle.

"You understand what you're saying, don't you? The accusation you're leveling at this ci—"

"I've leveled no accusations, Doctor. It is well known that Elendhaven's harbour was magic tainted for centuries before the founding of the town. If something's been pulled up from the depths—"

"—this city's economy depends on whale-oil exports, Herr Ambassador. If . . . were true . . ."

". . . by . . . der of the Cro . . ."

The voices passed from the stairwell. Johann had to lean his ear around the wall to catch the last strains of the conversation: Humours. Consultation. Sorcerer. He didn't hear the sound of footsteps approaching.

"Excuse me?"

Johann leapt to attention, spun on his heel to greet the interloper. It was the Ambassador's female companion, Eleanor, wearing a green tea gown and clutching a bundle of towels to her chest.

"Oh, I'm sorry," her voice fluttered. "I mistook you for an orderly."

Is that all? Johann thought. She caught him eavesdropping and yet her first assumption was that he—and his salt-stained coat—belonged here? He looked her over, intrigued by the way she shrank against her full height. She was practically quailing like a sparrow. And she *was* tall, even with her dark hair worn down around her shoulders.

Johann set his hands on his hips so that he could hide the stolen forceps behind the drape of his coat. The rail spike was still sitting in his pocket. "Really? Are hospital orderlies often known to wear sealskin?"

"I do not think so," she answered, utterly and tragically earnest. "But I am new to Elendhaven. Chopping up bodies is ugly enough work without the particular maladies that plague the North."

Johann hummed, running a thumb down the outline of the spike. "And what maladies would those be?"

"Frostbite. Marine parasites. I've heard there was a plague here not so many years ago." She set a finger to her bottom lip. "Have we met before?"

Up close, beneath the wash of yellow light, Johann noticed that her hands were much darker than her face. She wore greasepaint to disguise the hue of her skin. He swaggered a step forward and into a shallow mockery of a bow.

"We saw each other last week, near the town square. I'm Herr Leickenbloom's manservant."

Something surged through her expression, but it looked far more like confusion than recognition. "Of course," she said. "Herr Leickenbloom. He's peculiar, is he not? I met him for only a moment, but his manner seemed rather contradictory. Oh—" She shook her head, as if she had just walked through a sheet of cobweb. "I must apologize once again. I'm being terribly rude about your master."

"Don't worry about it." Johann laughed. "You don't know the half of how *peculiar* he is. He's also extremely particular, about time especially, so—" He swept past her, hands in his pockets, brushing the hard metal edges of his makeshift weapons. "I should be on my way."

He felt her eyes following him down the hallway. He was tempted to turn back to see what face she made when unexamined, but *that* would look suspicious.

"I'll see you again at Herr Leickenbloom's dinner?" she called after him.

Johann waved at her over his shoulder. "Oh," he called back, grinning at the adroitness of his own joke. "I *sincerely* doubt it."

– VI –

THE BLACK MOON

The restaurant Florian chose for his annual dinner was called Perle, and it served authentic Norden cuisine. Sticky oysters, purple-shelled crabs, black-water soup. Seal eyeballs in rendered whale fat, the only parts of them fit for eating. These parts were flash-fried, and sautéed with caramelized onions and red spice. The wine was so tart and dry that it left an aftertaste of hang-over vomit.

Before the dinner, Florian had dressed Johann with calculation. "Have you ever noticed," Florian asked him, "that when you walk down the street, people do not pay you much mind?"

Johann moved uncomfortably beneath Florian's deft fingers on his coat buttons. His arm was still sore from where Florian had put to use the fruits of his little shopping trip earlier. The gouge from the fleam had sealed over, but his veins were throbbing where the tourniquet had squeezed them taut. Nothing to show for it, but he imagined the damage it might have done to Florian's skinny little arm: bruises that would last for days. The leather of his gloves creaked when he flexed his hands. "It's something I work hard at," he replied. "I hide in the shadows. I am a shadow."

Florian lifted one pale eyebrow. "You are a sore thumb of a man. Tall as a signpost, thin, and conspicuously unnatural. And yet you are practically translucent."

Johann said nothing. He had never given it much mind except to congratulate himself on his powers of obfuscation. Florian knotted Johann's bow tie for him and then set to work on his face. He darkened Johann's pallid skin with rouge, painted his lips with rose dye, highlighted the contours of his eyes with earth-toned powders. "Eyes slide over you," Florian whispered, dabbing a damp cloth at the curve of Johann's throat. "Until you put your knife to their jugular. Let's make you tangible."

Tonight, Florian was wearing a river-blue justaucorps embroidered with delicate rust-gold filigree. His tricorn was set with orange jewels and a bouquet of blue-hawk feathers at the back. He was almost comically small under the bell flare of the coat. Florian often dressed as if to cocoon himself; he burrowed beneath layers of frill and finery. As far as Johann knew he'd been in that cocoon for fifteen years, waiting to emerge as something terrible and lovely.

He'd dressed Johann in burgundy and black—waistcoat, gentleman's vest, a smart silver chain looped through the top buttonhole and pinned with a ruby brooch at the shoulder. Johann was seated to Florian's left, a place that he was informed was both an honour and a sign of servitude. It usually sat empty at Leickenbloom affairs. Many of the guests were Norden elite: powdered men in grey suits and white-feathered caps who wore young women on their arms like accessories, the last profiteers of the oil trade. In contrast, the Suden- and Mittengelt ambassadorial staff wore bold colours—magenta and lime silks, diaphanous scarves with intricate flowers stitched against the grain of the fabric. "To demonstrate their mastery of the trade routes," Florian explained in a whisper as the guests poured in. "You couldn't get pink or pale green dyes in the North if you sold your children for them."

Florian introduced Johann as his *bodyguard*.

"Fascinating!" The Ambassador leant forward on his thick elbow and looked Johann up and down from waist to nose and back again. He swirled the wine in his glass with such delicate fervour that little pearl bubbles foamed around the circumference. "And how did you come to be hired?"

Beneath the Ambassador's analysis, Johann faltered. He wasn't used to speaking to anyone without the comforting weight of a knife in his sleeve. He glanced at Florian for assistance, but his "master" was engaged in demonstrating the proper evisceration of a crab to some narrow-boned foreign woman in a dark green floral gown.

"Well"—Johann rubbed the pads of his thumb and forefinger together—"I attempted to rob him in a back alley one night."

The Ambassador's eyelids fluttered in shock. He looked to his right—to his companion, Eleanor—and back again, making a real show of confusion. "I'm sorry, I'm not certain that I heard you correctly."

Eleanor laughed and tapped the Ambassador's arm playfully. "He is joking, surely. What a delightful sense of humour!"

"I don't joke," Johann said flatly. "I jumped him on his way home and threatened to slit his pretty neck if he didn't empty his purse for me. Instead, he offered me a salary!"

"Well, that is certainly—" The Ambassador paused and took a long sip of his frothed wine. "—an *interesting* hiring strategy."

"I'd heard much of the barbarism of the North," Eleanor agreed, "but I never imagined myself breaking bread with a genuine brigand!"

"I'm nothing so organized as a brigand." Johann laughed. "Brigands work in gangs. They have laws and rules. I'm more of a mons—"

Florian interrupted him smoothly. "Johann, *what* are

you telling these poor people?" He swirled his fork in the air and pointed it at Johann, a rubbery piece of crab flesh trembling on its tines.

"They wanted to know how we met"—Johann smiled, broad and toothy—"and how I came to be in your employ."

"I cannot see why. It's not a very interesting story." Florian sighed dramatically and popped the crab into his mouth.

"That's not what Johann was telling us." Eleanor clasped her hands together. "He said that he tried to *rob* you."

"Well, yes, but as you can see, he did not make a very efficient enterprise of it."

"And what, Herr Leickenbloom, is your side of the story?" The Ambassador poured himself another cup of wine.

"Hardly as engaging as you seem to be imagining it. Johann was an uneducated cobbler who had recently lost his job. He made a desperate jab at my purse strings and I decided to take him on as charity." Florian's lips quirked at the edge of his glass and he gestured to Johann's shoulders, cutting a line across them through the air. "He has no formal martial training, but you will agree that he boasts an imposing build."

Johann bristled under his expensive clothes and

twitched his fingers instinctively around the hilt of a butter knife. Florian seemed to have dragged him to dinner purely for his own amusement, a blatant exercise in debasement.

"How generous," Eleanor remarked, trailing a finger along the rim of her glass. The squeak her skin made against the gold trim rose above the murmur of conversation. "Ansley was correct in naming you the last true gentleman in Elendhaven."

"Where *is* Ansley?" Florian wondered with the expected dose of concern.

The Ambassador frowned. "He's entertaining one of Herr Charpentier's foreign investors tonight."

"Truly?" Florian replied in a toneless drawl. "They're attempting to secure a construction company without even knowing if the railroad can be fixed."

Johann rolled his eyes and began to flip the butter knife between two fingers. This sort of empty-headed conciliatory babble had bored him to begin with and only tortured him further the more he was exposed to it. It was, however, quite amusing to watch Florian pretend to give a shit while the Ambassador made an overplayed attempt at sympathetic piety.

"Why, that is quite the snub on Ansley's part, is it not?" he warbled. "How dire. I should have urged him to come."

Before Florian could respond, the waiter swept past

to whisper something in his ear. His expression changed subtly—almost imperceptibly—at whatever he was told. The smile moved a breadth from "polite" to "pleased." The waiter closed the doors to the private dining room and Florian rose to his feet and tapped his teaspoon against a glass, signaling that the champagne for the toast had been poured. The noise was a clear, cool ringing that hushed the heated and drunken conversation in the room immediately. All eyes went to their host.

Florian, wreathed luminous in orange light, raised his glass above his head, leading the table in a toast. The filigree of his coat burned the colour of an inferno. "It is good," he said, "to see equal numbers of familiar and unfamiliar faces tonight. As I am the last son of one of Elendhaven's great founding houses, it is important for me to take the lead when it comes to hosting dignitaries from our sister nations. In that light, it is my pleasure to treat all of you to this authentic Norden feast."

The guests clapped politely by rattling their jewelry.

"As many of you know, Elendhaven has a checkered history that is subject to wild and dark speculation among southerners. We struggle to disabuse our fellows of these myths. Thank you for joining me in this annual dinner in the spirit of cultural exchange. Especially tonight—the anniversary of our greatest and most . . . *personal* tragedy."

Johann's ears perked up at the dip Florian's honeyed voice took on the word "personal." He dangled the knife between thumb and forefinger and watched Florian through veiled eyes. Across the table, Eleanor from the South was leaning forward in her chair, lips pursed with sympathetic curiosity. The Ambassador had gone sombre.

"Those who lived through the troubles will remember—fifteen years ago, the people of Elendhaven suffered through a terrible plague. The illness swept first through our gutters, then through the factory districts. Its maw was so ravenous that its teeth were at the throats of even our most privileged, sheltered citizens. My own family fell victim to the nameless plague. My parents, both my uncles, their wives, and all of their children. My . . ." He paused a moment before continuing, his gaze floating towards the ceiling.

"If even the Leickenblooms—who have stood in this city since time immemorial—could fall victim to this disease, they said, what hope had the rest of the city to stand against it? Indeed, all of Elendhaven would have fallen into the Nord Sea and our rotted flesh been consumed by the crustaceans, had it not been for aid from the Great Kingdoms of Mittengelt. Your people rode to our aid like the knights of old, wielding your gold and doctors. And for that, I toast you."

He raised his cup, a brilliant and altogether fake smile lighting his features. The pink wine glimmered jewel bright, but Florian did not put the glass to his lips. He held his pose—a prince triumphant painted in classical oils, rich and aqueous and just the slightest bit smudged around the edges—and he watched every single puffed-up noble at the table down their drinks. As soon as the champagne passed their lips, Florian's polite mask fell away.

"Of course," he sneered, "your aid came only when our gates were barred with corpses. Your aid came only when you feared that we would no longer be fit to deliver whale oil for your lamps or oysters for your feasts. Your aid came only when our silver mines closed because the miners were too sick to work. You came to save us only when you thought you might own us in return. And now you come running back, when it looks as if the mines may flourish once again."

Johann eased back in his chair and watched the faces around him twitch first in confusion, then in outrage. The silk-drenched man to Johann's left sputtered into his ascot, but no words formed on his lips. His eyes rolled back and he fainted face-first into his soup, splattering Johann's coat. The Sudengelt Ambassador was panicking, eyes darting wildly as his compatriots began to flinch and vomit. Eleanor swayed in her seat and slumped onto his shoulder. Florian fished out his napkin and leant forward to wipe the foamy spittle from the Ambassador's mouth with a kindness that might have been sincere.

"I am a brother who loved," Florian said, "and I can attest that there is no brotherly love between Elendhaven and the South, or the Old Kingdoms. For the true sons and daughters of Elendhaven, our mother is the sea and our sister is the winter. We stand alone at the edge of the world, as I stood alone atop the corpses of my family. When you go forth from this city, you will bring the same ruin to your people that you allowed to befall mine. I am Hallandrette's favourite son and I will devour your bones as surely as she does when her unloved children are cast into the ocean."

When the last man fell unconscious, Johann stood and clapped. "Encore!" he shouted. Florian shot him a flat look. "I didn't know you were a lyricist, Herr Leickenbloom."

"Don't start."

"You don't expect me to believe that you said all that off the cuff. You've been practising that for years, haven't you? Perhaps in the mirror?"

Florian ignored him. He was unpacking needles and vials and cloth. "Make sure the door is locked. We have work to do."

While Johann locked the door, Florian swirled about

the room and tapped various guests on the top of the head as if he were playing duck-duck-goose.

"Take their blood," he said.

"Want me to swipe their gold rings while I'm down here? I know a few ways to make a man piss himself while asleep—"

"I told you not to start."

Johann did as he was told and retrieved the blood from Florian's chosen subjects. Across the room, Florian was holding a vial of cloudy grey liquid up to a candle, brow furrowed.

"What"—Johann pressed down on an unconscious courtier's vein to slow the bleeding—"exactly are we doing again?"

"Honestly, Johann, do you listen to a word I say?" Florian sighed. "I am doing what I've promised. I'm going to show you what the plague does. I've several strains to test, and just as many *willing* test subjects."

Into the half-sipped champagne glass of every second guest went a drop of plague. When the work was finished, Florian went back to his seat and held his own glass aloft. "One final toast," he said, and hit his spoon to the glass rim.

At the sound of the chime, the nobles began to wake, pulling themselves to consciousness like newborn calves stumbling into the morning light. The man who had fallen in his soup shook the oyster meat from his beard as if nothing unusual had happened. The Ambassador groaned into his palm, his eyes scrunched up with all the telltale signs of a hangover.

"—as was the first toast, the last toast is to you, who have so enthusiastically celebrated with me what is usually a dark mark on my calendar. Thank you, sincerely, from the bottom of my heart."

This time, Florian tipped back his glass and drank the champagne. So did everyone else in the room except for, Johann noticed, the fair Eleanor, who simply twirled the thin spine of her glass between her blunt fingers, a strange expression on her face.

The party wound itself down soon afterwards, the consensus among the courtiers and politicians being that the wine had been so strong as to cloud their senses. "A wild dinner party," said one, "for such a dour occasion." "Is this how tragedies are always celebrated in the North?" wondered another.

Florian instructed Johann to show the guests out. Johann unlocked the door and stood straight-backed, doing his very best impression of a footman and trying not to smile.

As she passed by, Eleanor—carrying her high-heeled

shoes in one hand, a jewel-studded purse in the other—stopped for a moment. She stared at Johann hard for several seconds as she swayed on her bare feet.

"Can I help you?" he asked.

She blinked and something lit in her dark eyes. She opened her mouth as if to speak but seemed to think better of it. Instead, she shook her head and dipped down to slip back into her shoes. Johann watched the shape of her stumble her way towards the front of the restaurant.

*   *   *

When the door to Leickenbloom Manor slammed shut, Florian began laughing. "I can't—" He hiccuped. "I *can't believe* that it worked. I waded neck-deep into the abyss, and I *took* hold of it! I wielded it like a *tool!*"

He spun into the drawing room, with his arms flailing wide, and fell into his favourite armchair. He kicked out one slender leg and rubbed his palm over his eyes, failing to stow the tide of his mirth.

Johann leant against the door and watched his "employer" with veiled fascination. Florian radiant was almost a different man from the dour, sharp-tongued businessman who went to and from the manor each day. Unhinged and cackling at his own wit, his hair mussed and his cheeks spotting red, he looked half his age. He looked softer, more breakable. Like a child who had never been kissed, never been smacked with an open palm.

"How long will it take them to die?" Johann asked.

"Oh, who *knows.* That's the delightful part, don't you think? This is only my trial run—who can tell how it will unfold from here?" Florian's fingers fumbled on the top button of his coat. His hands were shaking and blue at the tips, numb and clumsy from too much sorcery.

Johann crossed the room in three easy strides and knelt at Florian's feet. "You complain about people treating you like a bauble and you can't even undress yourself."

"Shut up, Johann," Florian said, but he dropped his hands and surrendered his buttons to Johann's long fingers.

"So. You had . . . a sibling?"

The muscles in Florian's shoulders went tense, and Johann felt his heart quicken under his fingers.

"Don't get worked up, Florian. I'd already snooped around enough to guess at such a thing—her name was Flora, right? Lovely little Norden girl with fluffy yellow hair. Your perfect mirror. A twin?"

"I . . . yes." Florian swallowed hard and allowed Johann to help him shrug out of his coat. "You've guessed correctly. But I don't say her name, and neither should you."

"Why not?"

"I've erased her from the memory of everyone who would have known her. If you said her name in the wrong company it would—" Florian's good mood had evaporated. He made a frustrated noise in the back of his throat and set the sole of his left boot on Johann's chest. "It is better that Elendhaven forget the particulars of how my family died. Help me out of my boots."

Johann ran a thumb along the curve of Florian's delicate ankle. "Only if you explain yourself," he hummed, looking up at Florian beneath the shadows of his hair.

"Nonsense. Oh, don't be difficult, Johann. I've already explained more than you're owed." Florian ground his heel into Johann's collarbone, but he was not nearly strong enough to inflict any harm. Johann caught his foot by the heel and pulled it to the side. He began unlacing the boot with a grin.

"Come on, sugarsnap, you *want* to tell me. You've never told anyone about this, have you?"

"I've whispered it to the dark," Florian hissed, "which is the only confessor I need."

"I am the dark, Herr Leickenbloom. You can tell me anything you want."

"Is that supposed to impress me?"

"Don't pretend that your melodramatic ego isn't flattered by the idea that I might exist to soothe your broken psyche." Johann smoothly slid off one boot and began to unlace the other.

Florian sighed and covered his eyes with the back of his hand. "My father caught the plague first, as he was always visiting the textile mills. He liked to envision himself as the sort of manager that peasants admired, that they spoke of fondly to their children: 'Ah, Herr Leickenbloom is so kind, darlings. Today he slipped a silver coin into my palm, when he saw that my knees were shaking. He smiled at me when he told me I couldn't leave work early, even when I coughed blood onto the sleeve of my tunic.' He was the first noble in Elendhaven to get sick, so of course everyone thought—" Florian laughed darkly to himself.

"What did they think?"

"My family was once known to be filthy with powerful sorcerers. My house was founded in the Dark Ages, when magic was the key to power. Of course, after so many generations of intermarriage with other noble houses, our magical blood began to sour, but stories still propagated about our household. When my grandmother noticed her first son show signs of arcane aptitude, she picked him up by his chubby little legs and dashed his head against the stones in our garden. She told me this story proudly. Told me that she scrubbed his brains from between the grooves of our back step herself. Still . . . when my father's skin began to blister, people began to *talk*."

Johann undid the silk bow at the top of Florian's boot and dipped his thumbs under the lip of the leather. "They blamed the Leickenblooms for the plague?"

"They barricaded us in our home," Florian hissed. "Until we were all dead, save for me. On the mere suspicion—the *absolutely baseless suspicion*—that one of us might have been a sorcerer! Well, I decided that if Elendhaven wanted to see a *magical plague* so badly, I would do my best to show them one. And I see no rea-son to stop there. The landed gentry, the emissaries from Mittengelt, the southerners who stole our futures and picked our bones . . . no one is blameless."

"The suspicion wasn't baseless, though. One of you *was* a sorcerer." Johann trailed his fingers down the back of Florian's silk stocking as he pulled his leg free of the boot. "They weren't wrong."

Florian reared up in his seat, furious. "How *dare* you—!"

"It's funny, don't twist my words—these assholes signed their own death warrant, but Florian: *they weren't wrong*. They feared that the Leickenblooms were harbour-ing a magical child, a monster who would unleash a plague on them. Here you are."

"This game of deliberately provoking me has become *tiresome*, Johann. I don't understand what you gain from it."

Johann looked at the arc of Florian's pale throat, and the golden gashes his eyelids made when he blinked them shut. He hooked one of Florian's wrists with his thumb. He kissed the Leickenbloom family ring with the affection of fealty. Then he kissed Florian's knuckles, carefully and one at a time. He kissed the center of Florian's palm wet and said, "You're quite charming, you know, especially when you don't mean to be."

Florian's breathing hitched and he stared at Johann with impossibly bright eyes. After a moment, he yanked his hand away. "Stop this now," he said. He stood and headed for the stairs. Johann was taller and faster, and he caught Florian by the arm. He tucked him beneath his chin. "C'mon, Florian. You're so lonely. You live in a mausoleum. Surely a bachelor of your age has desires. *Needs*."

Florian squirmed in his grasp. "Let go of me."

Johann scraped his fingernails down the length of Florian's throat. He ran his thumb over the lump in Florian's jugular. "But that's not the reason you're a bachelor, is it?"

"Don't—"

"No, no—I have this one figured out." Johann kissed Florian's jaw, fingers tight around his throat. "There isn't anyone else, is there? There isn't a woman in the world who can measure up to *Flora*."

Florian shivered and made a weak attempt to escape. "I will only warn you once, Johann."

"I'm sure you will," Johann purred. He tightened his grip on Florian's throat, indented his esophagus softly and sweetly, just like a kiss. Florian's breath guttered inside his throat. His eyes rolled back as Johann pressed hard enough to leave long, worm-shaped bruises on his skin. Florian's breath spooled out of him inch by inch, like a ribbon pulled from his mouth. Johann put his lips to the crown of Florian's head and eased his palm back, rocking his hand, wrenching it around the delicate cartilage in measured strokes.

The tingle started at the inside of his wrist, like someone had pressed at the tangle of capillary veins. The feeling itched and forced open the claw of his hand. The pressure crawled through his bones and trickled into his fingers until his hand flung out to the side. The force inhabited his entire body and, against his will, Johann released Florian and reeled back. He tried to fight against it, but it was like his joints were on invisible strings; every motion he made snapped back against itself twofold. He slammed himself against the wall. Twice. Three times, before crashing to the floor.

Florian bent forward, gasping and pawing at his neck

88

and mouth. He wheeled around and glared down at Johann. There was no fear rattling in his expression—rather, he looked *irritated,* as if Johann had merely inconvenienced him by nearly strangling him to death.

"I *told* you," Florian rasped. "Johann, you *never* listen. You want to see what my magic can do? You're asking for an intimate *demonstration?*"

Florian raised his hands like a conductor and Johann felt his own fingers move against him to clamp tightly around his neck. They cranked tight as vices and they wrung and wrested until something snapped and everything went black and empty inside his head.

When he gasped back to life, Florian was above him, eyes hard and devoid of emotion. His hair was a circle of fire in the lamplight.

"You obey my desires, Johann. It does not work in reverse."

"Right," Johann gasped.

"Is that clear?"

"As glass, Herr Leickenbloom."

A very small, very cruel smile quirked the corner of Florian's mouth. Slowly, he sank to his knees and pressed a soft, trembling kiss to Johann's lips. "Good," he whispered. "I needed to make certain that you understood the distinction."

– VII –

FLORA

When Florian was ten he and his twin sister, Flora, walked the entire length of the Black Crescent in the dead of a winter's night. Flora's hair was three inches longer and she often wore skirts, but otherwise there was no difference between them. She wanted to comb the beach and look at aberrations. "No one practises looking at them," she said, "and so they can't see them when they walk among us." Florian had no trouble seeing aberrants, but no one in his family ever talked about why. Flora did not like that there was a part of her brother's life that she could not touch.

"I wonder if anyone's ever found one shaped like a person," she said, touching the slick skin of a beached shark.

"That's not possible, Flora," Florian told her snottily. "It affects seals and sharks because the seals and sharks live in the ocean."

"Yes, but what if you threw someone in?" Flora's wheat-coloured hair shone in the moonlight. "I hear that they throw prostitutes and orphans into the water."

"After they've died," Florian pointed out.

"But what if they weren't dead yet? Then they'd come back all mutated and strange." She kicked the shark and Florian winced, because he had heard stories about dead whales exploding on the shore. "And no one would know, because they can't remember. Except you, Florian."

He took her arm and pulled her away from the corpse. "Why are you so obsessed by this, Flora?" He sighed. She whipped around and gazed at him with wide eyes gleaming and knife sharp in the silver light.

"I want to know everything Grandmother won't talk about. If you walk into dark places, I want to be with you. If I die"—she took a deep breath—"throw me into the sea, Florian, and I will come back to you."

"Don't be ridiculous, Flora. You won't die." Florian wrapped his arms around his sister and buried his nose in her sweet-smelling hair. "I plan for us both to live forever."

* * *

Johann walked the coastline, whistling to himself. Since the dinner party, Florian had taken to sleeping until noon, waking to the tea and croissants he had Johann fetch him every morning. He wasn't polite about it either. Florian hadn't had servants since he was a young boy, but Johann suspected he'd treated the help poorly as a child, too. Surely he was just as rude and puffed up then, all self-righteous in plaid overalls and silk ribbons. The thought made Johann chuckle, and he ghosted the tips of his gloved fingers across the length of his neck. Of course, he did not bruise, or scar, but the memory of the wound remained like a collar.

A woman stood where the shore began to curve. She was dressed in a long brown coat and she had waded ankle-deep into the black water. As Johann approached her, he recognized the glass-sharp cheekbones and the night-coloured hair—it was the southern woman, Eleanor, for once off the arm of her Ambassador. She wore no greasepaint that morning and her thick hair was pulled over one shoulder in a loose braid.

She did not turn to look at Johann as he passed her. Her eyes rolled to the side before her attention returned to the horizon. Johann remembered what Florian said about him—tall as a signpost, practically translucent—so he stopped, picked up a large, round stone, and threw it into the water. In the silence of a windless morning, the sound was loud as a musket. Eleanor gasped and turned to him.

"Wakey, wakey," Johann said. He grinned, tried to look charming. As he looked at her now, without all the glamour and pretension, she was really quite beautiful with her long, narrow face and her russet skin. Without the artificial colouring, the natural darkness of her eyes and lips was apparent—Johann thought her Florian's complement, this mature and poised statue of a woman who minced and tittered falsely.

She tipped her head and examined Johann with a piercing gaze. "Excuse me," she said, "but have we met?"

Johann almost replied, *More than once, you stupid bint,* but thought better of it. Instead, he said, "You know, the water is poison. You'll catch something nasty if you stand in it all day, even in your boots."

Eleanor brushed her braid over one shoulder and took two steps back onto the shore. "Ah, I see. I'm from the South—much farther south, I mean, than the Mittengelt provinces."

"The . . . colonies?" Johann ventured. He'd heard of the southern colonies in the papers, but they were so far away that they might as well not exist. Who could imagine a land with no winter?

Eleanor nodded. "Where I'm from, the water is so clear that you can see the seabed on a bright day. It's so warm that you can bathe babies in it and only worry about the salt. I'd read about the horrors of the Nord Sea, but there are some things that only become real once you see them."

She ducked down and plucked a hallanroe stone from the sand. She placed it in the center of her palm and held it out to Johann. "You are from Elendhaven, correct?"

"Lady, I *am* Elendhaven." She raised an eyebrow. "I mean"—Johann swept into a shallow bow—"that of all the people from Elendhaven you'll ever meet, you'll probably never meet anyone as from Elendhaven as I am."

"Somehow—" Eleanor winced and pressed her free palm to her head, as if something sharp had shot through between her eyes. It passed quickly. "Somehow I . . . knew that. Are you certain we've never met?"

"I'm certain that you seem to be certain that we've never met."

"That isn't any kind of answer, sir."

Johann grew bold and stepped close to her. He tapped the stone in her palm. Her hands were rough—far more calloused than any fine lady's hands had business being. Even Florian—whose arms were cracked black with arcane cysts, who did horrible work with his own hands— had palms as soft as milk.

"You want to ask me what this is, don't you?"

"I've heard the name: hallanroe. There is a statue of Hallandrette in the city square—I was curious about the myth behind the stones."

Johann snatched the stone from her palm, tossed it in

the air, and caught it, holding it up between two fingers so that it aligned with her eyes.

"If you lose something important," he said, "you throw what you lost in the sea. Then you find one of these, and hatch from it a little slave, all for yourself, to do whatever you want with."

Eleanor's pretty mouth twisted as she stared at the stone. It was so white that the light hurt the eyes where it curved. "In a city like this," she murmured, "I could believe a story like that has some truth to it."

"'A city like this,'" Johann echoed. "What's a lady like you doing here anyway?"

She laughed, but not kindly. "Believe it or not, I'm hunting something." She patted down her thigh, and for the first time Johann noticed the pistol hanging at her belt. "I'm looking for a sorcerer."

*　*　*

When their father developed boils on his lip, he hid away in his study, did all his correspondence from home. He hoped he might weather the illness without word spreading. Sometimes, if the right oils and teas were applied during the early stages, the plague would pass and the victim would recover. Not for the Leickenbloom family.

It was a maid—or a cook, maybe the footman, one of the help anyway—who betrayed them, went crying in some pub downtown about how the witchy Leickenblooms had brought doom to the town once again. Foolish of them; the townsfolk trapped the servants in with the family, and Frau Leicken-bloom locked every single one of them in the cellar without food or drink.

When the pounding under the floorboards stopped, their mother said, "Good riddance," and adjusted the fringe of her shawl. She didn't cry when she threw her husband's corpse down with them, either. That night, however, she started coughing, and didn't stop.

"It's in her leg," Flora said when their mother did not wake up the next day. Flora was hitched up on the bed, roll-ing up Mother's sleep-clothes as Florian listened to her heart-beat. It was faint but steady.

"I heard in school that if you can cut off the limb the plague began in, you can stop it from spreading. See here." Flora tapped their mother's left leg. "Her foot is black, and it's all up this leg, to the knee. But not the other one."

Florian did not think that was true, but he could not ar-gue with Flora. She was the sun and he was the moon. He receded whenever she shone bright, as sure as the passing of night into day.

"If it spreads up to her thigh we can't do anything, because that's where the big vein is. The one that kills you if you prick it."

"I read that there are three big veins in the leg," Florian mumbled, like reciting equations. He wanted to be a doctor someday. "The iliac, the femoral, and the saphenous. The last one runs all the way down, Flora."

She sighed. "You know what I mean. She won't bleed to death if we cauterize it quickly, right?"

"I . . . I think that's how it works, yes."

"Stoke the fireplace, Florian; then use your sorcery to make her calm. I'm going to get a hatchet from the cellar."

Where the servants died, neither of them said. *Where Father's body is.*

Flora's pink tongue peeked out from between her lips as she heated the hatchet blade. Florian watched her face in the flames, holding tight to his mother's wrist. His mother was a cold woman, strict and pinched, but her skin was warm as a boiled egg just out of the pot. He wondered if it was the fever or if she'd always been this warm-blooded. He could not remember ever being held by her.

The blade steaming, Flora staggered to her feet, dragged down by the weight of the axe head. "Hold her steady, baby brother."

Florian panicked. "W-we should move her to the floor. We need a . . . a stable surface. The mattress w-will absorb some of the blow. It won't . . . it won't be a clean cut."

Flora stared at him. Florian clarified, dumbly, "It needs to be a clean cut, Flora."

"Yeah . . . I know."

As Flora's brow creased and the axe blade cooled, Florian took hope. Maybe Flora would change her mind with so many obstacles.

"Okay . . . okay, take her shoulders. I'll get her feet."

Of course she wouldn't change her mind. Flora was so stubborn it was an affliction. They moved their mother to the floor and Flora took the hatchet back to the fireplace, just to be safe. It was too heavy for her, so heavy that it took her three tries to raise it above her head. Florian held his mother's hand tight enough that his fingernails drew blood. She began to stir from exposure to the hearth's heat and the pinch of her son's desperate grasp. Florian tried to focus his power, to flood her mind with calm. But how could he make her calm when he was falling apart?

In the moment the hatchet dropped, her eyes flew open.

It was not a clean cut. The hatchet stuck in the tibia, and Flora was not strong enough to tear it free. Blood burst up from the saphenous vein in tall ribbons that throbbed in time with their mother's heartbeat. Fast, like a caged butterfly, then slower, and slower. The first spurt caught Flora in the eye, and she fell back on her bottom.

Their mother screamed at a terrible, ragged frequency. It was an animal noise, the kind of noise a human can only make when they see the other side of the abyss. Flora was shouting, too. "Florian! Fl-Florian, d-do something!"

He did the only thing he could. He put his hands on his mother's face and used his power to burn the inside of her skull to ash through her eye sockets. He had never used magic so freely. It tore through him, rippling beneath his skin in sharp, cruel waves. He screwed his eyes shut, bit the inside of his cheek, dug his fingers so hard a thumb slipped into her eye socket. His mouth filled with the taste of copper. It stung like a burst pox mark, made his veins feel like they were filling up with boiled mercury: hot and vicious and deadly.

When Florian pulled back, his mother looked calm. Pristine, except for her black eyes. The stream of blood became a trickle.

She was already dead when we came to see her, *Florian thought.* We offered her a mercy. She didn't go slow like Father did. She would have hated to go like that. It was important to Mother to be beautiful.

When Florian looked up, he saw that Flora's bedclothes were all askew. The clasp of her nightgown had fallen open to reveal a black scab in the hollow where her neck dipped in to meet her collarbone. He reached out to touch it, knowing that his face told her exactly what he saw.

Finally, her bravado cracked. She threw herself into Florian's arms and began to sob. Flora did not let anyone see her cry, disdained anything that could be construed as girlish fragility. But there was no one left to hear her but Florian. The twins, alone in a house of ghosts, held each other until the fire died and their mother's blood congealed on the carpet.

"Florian, stay with me until the end," she begged, rubbing her snotty nose all over his bedclothes.

He answered, "Where would I go?"

* * *

"Florian?"

No answer. Johann snapped the front door shut behind him and swept in through the foyer, searching for any sign of his master. The sitting room, the grand hall, the kitchen . . . Florian was in none of his usual haunts: not the bedroom nor the office nor the library. It seemed like a new locked door opened every day in Leickenbloom Manor now that mischief and dark sorcery had thawed out the long winter of its master's depression.

"Florian! I need to talk to you!"

Johann's voice echoed off the narrow walls, the tall ceilings; it slithered down the whole yawning length of the main hall and bounced back to him. He stopped at the edge of the very rich—and very dusty—woven rug that tracked from one end of the hall to the other. To his left was Florian's bedroom, to his right a peeling impressionist portrait of the manor from when it was first built.

For some reason, his toe hesitated when he attempted to nudge it over the line.

Florian forbade me, his bones said. *Well, fuck him,* his brain replied. But still, he found that he could not move. He stood like that—one heel raised, his hand on the wall, eyebrows furrowed—not feeling the seconds click by despite the clock ticking at the end of the hall. He felt something peculiar rise inside of him—something old and glassy, familiar like a song heard from behind a closed window. Johann remembered ... *a corpse, spit up by the tide, caught on a serrated outcropping of rock by a fold of pale, pimpled skin. It was leaking a thread of yellow bile; bloated, foaming, a slick sheen of fat ... black growths bubbling up where the skin gathered. The Thing knelt beside it and examined it for minutes. Hours. Before he had a name he—*

"Johann." Florian's voice broke the spell of memory. Johann looked up to see his *master* standing at the other end of the hall, hands on his hips and head tipped to one side. "How long have you been standing there?"

Johann's eyes flickered towards the clock, read the position of the hour hand with dismay that he hoped did not show on his face. *Two hours.* He smirked and said out loud, "Five minutes. Didn't you hear me hollering?"

Florian stared at him a moment longer than was comfortable, as if he was trying to solve Johann's equation, searching for a lie in his tone. Johann slipped his hands into his pockets and slouched casually, raising his eyebrows in a manner that invited inquiry. *C'mon, dewdrop, why would I lie about something stupid like this?*

Florian sighed and brushed past him. "I was in the library."

"Really? I checked there."

"The *other* library," Florian said, untucking a very old book from beneath his elbow. "The private one. It is very well insulated. Why didn't you come to find me?"

"I didn't—"

Florian did not wait for his explanation. "It doesn't matter," he chirped. "Follow me. I've something to show you."

Johann's heart thumped and he spun on his heel to follow Florian like a dog. Things had changed between them since the night of the dinner party. Johann had never fucked someone more than once, and had certainly never fucked someone slowly or ponderously, as anything but opportunistic—and often unsatisfying—curiosity. He'd never met a person who remembered he existed five minutes after turning away from him, or who cared to learn what he was called.

Johann had always thought himself an exceptional reader of people. You can learn a lot about someone's inner life if allowed to examine them the way their shadow does—close enough to breathe down their neck, but unnoticed, unremarked upon, *invisible*. But Florian watched back; he learned, adjusted, and could predict Johann's movements and moods now. A strange thing, to be studied like a pinned moth. Acceptable only because Florian was not quite human, either, was he? Something inside him burned brighter. *A curiosity*, he had called himself before, *in a glass jar*. If only he knew how true that was. Johann could not help but look at him with eyes coated in glass—curious and shining, refracted endlessly into split images of light. Was this what it meant to know something else's name?

They went down, down farther into the house than Johann had ever been. Florian carried a heavy set of iron keys at his belt and used three of them as they went, pausing to rattle through the artefacts with the caged patience of someone who has got almost everything they want. He led Johann down a spiral staircase of uneven stone. The crisp chill that hung in the air turned damp as they descended into the basement. The scent of metal and mold clung to the cracks in the wall.

At the bottom was an ancient cellar, carved into the bedrock beneath the mansion and surely a hundred years older than it. The pillars that supported it were hunched with age, giving the room a disarming shape that tricked the eyes when viewed from the center. A flick of Florian's smallest finger filled the room with dancing orange light that cast ghost-shadows on the black walls.

"This is it," Florian said as he stepped off the last stair. He'd laid out his laboratory along the walls: wooden tables filled with brass instruments that held vials of blood, samples of seal fat, and, simmering above an open flame, something viscous, black, and foul. Florian set his book down with a thump that rattled the hollow glass. Johann stepped over the remnants of a paint inscription on the ground as he passed beneath the room's keystone. His eyes traced the edges of the drawing, trying to divine its shape. It was smudged at the center and so old that the humidity had burned the skeleton of it into the floor forever.

"As I was saying upstairs"—Johann skulked around the wide end of the room, sticking to the shadows on instinct—"we've got a problem."

"Oh?" Florian hummed as he checked his equipment, paying Johann no heed at all.

"A . . . a Mage Hunter, is that what you call them?" Johann braced his elbow on the far end of the wooden counter and leant into it, watching Florian work. "Woman with a pistol, seems to know *about* you, if not . . . about *you.* The Ambassador's ornamental woman; she's been undercover this whole time."

"Ah yes," Florian replied. "She didn't drink the second toast. I thought that was odd."

Johann flattened his brow. "You *knew*?"

"Well, I suspected. But I passed by her near the market yesterday and she did not spare me a second glance. She's quite good, but if she were smart I would have been her first suspect. It's unfortunate that she attended that dinner, but if we take special care to keep out from under her nose from now on, I'll do my best to make sure that she doesn't think anything about me at all."

"You could have told me," Johann pouted.

Florian snorted. "And, pray tell, what difference would that have made?"

"I could have"—Johann pulled the tip of his thumb across his neck—"taken care of it for you."

Florian brushed the idea off with a dismissive hand gesture. "Don't be ridiculous. If you had killed her they would have sent a dozen more. Besides, I'm almost finished."

"Finished with what? Your *special* project?"

Florian gestured for Johann to come closer. Johann obeyed, hovering over his shoulder like a gargoyle. "See this blood?" Florian pointed to one of the vials at the center of his collection. It was darker than the other samples, almost black. The surface of the blood had grown a thick membrane of clot the texture of a scab.

"That's not how it normally ages."

Florian tapped the vial and the blood jumped. "Blood need not die when it leaves the body. In the right hands, it can survive to tell you many things." He glanced at Johann and flashed a brilliant, mischievous grin. "Herr Ambassador's delegation was meant to head back to Mittengelt this week, but I've heard that he's holed up in his rooms and has not seen or spoken to any of his aides in nearly three days."

"And this . . . is his blood."

"Mmm. His blood, riddled with plague but still alive. I'm still several steps from where I wish to be." He opened his dusty old book and thumbed through the pages. "My grandmother once told me that there were traces of magical theory hidden in our family heirlooms."

"The same grandmother who bashed her son's head against the garden wall?" Johann wondered with a drawl. He went to touch one of the vials, but Florian slapped his hand away.

"She'd gone senile in her old age. Either she called me Flora or she called me by her own son's name, but she never recognized the magic in me. And so she told me many useful things. I think . . . hm, I think I've identified the cipher, but I'm missing all the keys." Florian leant forward, a knuckle on his chin, to examine the blackened blood. "I need you to do a favour for me," he said.

Johann slithered up behind him and wound his arms around his waist. He nudged his nose beneath the soft curtain of Florian's hair and found the pulse at his neck.

"Ask me nicely," he whispered. Florian jerked back his elbow to throw Johann off, but it was a weak gesture, perfunctory. All a part of the song and dance.

"I *was* asking nicely," Florian bit out, going still beneath Johann's hands. Johann dug his fingers in deep and spun Florian around, pinning him against the edge of the table, one palm set to either side of his rib cage. The vials rattled violently.

"*Nicer*, then." Johann dipped down to kiss him, relishing the way Florian still trembled a little—entirely unbidden—when they were close.

Florian turned his mouth away. "D-don't," he stuttered, "d-don't. Th-the glass will break—"

"Well, that's entirely in your hands, isn't it, sugarsnap?" Johann purred, brushing back Florian's hair. "Nothing gets broken if you don't struggle."

The words sat between them for a few moments. Florian met his eyes steadily, a defiant set to his jaw that didn't reach the rest of his face. He didn't pull away when Johann tried to kiss him this time—he opened his mouth under it. Johann bit into him, devoured him. Florian hooked a hand around his neck and fumbled the other one into his pocket as Johann slipped his long fingers beneath one knee and hiked him up onto the worktable.

"I told you . . . to mind the . . . the glass—" Florian hissed between kisses.

Johann slammed his hand down beside his thigh, pushed the ancient book aside to make room. "That's *your* responsibility," Johann reminded him.

Florian yanked something from his pocket as he got kissed again and scrabbled his hand against Johann's chest. "Take this—"

Johann pulled back, but not far enough to cool the breath between them. He snapped the object from Florian's hand and looked at it. A slip of paper—perfumed, dyed, no seal—with an address on it. "What do you want me to do with it?"

Florian smiled slyly and tossed his head, just enough to show an inch of pale skin above the frill of his collar. "I want you to fetch me back Grandmother's silverware."

* * *

When Flora died, he dragged her down the hall. Down the stairwell, down two whole flights into the front foyer. The air in the house was thick and foul. It took Florian an hour to hack one of the windows open with the bloodstained hatchet.

It was harder work to pull Flora's corpse through the garden. An early frost had turned all the grass and nettles hard and sharp. They caught on her dress and filled her tangled hair with brambles. The moon made her skin look transparent, as if she were already a ghost. Only her weight in his arms was corporeal.

In children, the blisters formed mostly on the chest and stomach. They rarely climbed past the collarbone. Flora's neck was swollen black and blue, but her face was unmarred. She looked like she was sleeping. Florian had kissed her cold lips, just to see if she would wake up, like a maiden in a Mittengelt fairy tale. Of course he knew it would not work. The middle kingdoms had forgotten the old ways. It would take a northern fairy tale to bring Flora back to him.

Because he loved her, he did as she had asked and took her corpse to the sea. He stuffed the body in a wheelbarrow and covered it with the blanket she slept with every night. She was heavy, as heavy as he was, so the trip to the docks was hard going. It was a quiet night; all the sailors and dock men were hiding in their tin-roof shacks with the blinds drawn shut to protect their families against the Wizard Baron's plague. Florian and Flora could have been the only two people left in the entire world. Maybe he had willed everyone else out of existence.

Before he tipped the barrow over, he knelt down to whisper in her ear, "I told you, Flora. We'll both live forever."

He watched the waves lap over her white face until the tide carried her out. It gulped her down, swallowed her whole. It was not the first time he'd watched a body disappear like that.

* * *

The monster of Elendhaven's nights waited until the streets were as black as oil before he slinked into the alley behind Ansley's rented town house. It was easy to climb the slick wall, digging his knife into the crumbling mortar and his fingers into the nicks in the bricks themselves. He hung off the top ledge of the sill and ran a long, thin needle through the seam where the window closed, lifting the lock from the outside. When he pulled open the frosted glass, a wave of stale air hit him in the face, and he recoiled in shock—it stank like a latrine on a summer afternoon.

He plugged his nose theatrically as he stepped in through the window, although there was no one to watch him. Well, wasn't that how it had been most of his life? Spinning a myth around himself even though no one was ever watching? It felt good in a perverse way to know that he had someone waiting at home who would be impressed by his impeccable performance. Who would pat his head and tell him that he did good. Like a dog, *heh*. Johann licked the last of Florian's taste out of his mouth and kicked open the door to Ansley's drawing room.

The suite was all gold-flecked floral patterns and low-burning kerosene lamps. Purple drapes with puffy chiffon stuffed between the layers. Silkfur-thread carpeting and ancient oak furniture plundered from the abandoned mansions of ruined nobles long since moved to Mittengelt. The center table had feet carved to look like the hooves of the boars that once roamed the mountainside. A fossil from a different age. Johann wondered if it had once resided in Leickenbloom Manor as well. Fitting that there was detritus of Florian's family scattered in every corner of the city, like bone and blood when a head is blown open by pistol fire.

Johann waltzed the circumference of the room, tapping all the paintings, just because he could. Florian had said that Ansley likely kept his family's heirlooms tucked away in the cellar, but Johann found what he was looking for sitting pretty on a mantelpiece: a set of hand-wrought silver dinnerware. Each piece was stamped with the same seal Florian wore on his left hand. Johann picked a plate up and tipped it towards the light. The mural carved into it depicted the mouth of the harbour as a gate and, above it, the sun. He noticed that it was dented near the top, so he set his thumb in the depression and made a gouging motion. It gave way beneath his finger. A high yield of silver, nearly pure.

He hummed to himself as he swept the dinnerware into his satchel. Quick work, and easy, too, but on his way back to the window something stalled him in his tracks: a tow of curiosity as strong as the tide at daybreak. Why did Ansley's impeccably decorated house stink worse than a beached seal? He remembered something Herr Charpentier had said the day they met: *You'd think he'd have the decency to share since you're putting them up.* The Ambassador was here, laid up with Florian's pernicious little germs.

Johann wanted to see it. No, he *needed* to see it, see what Florian Leickenbloom had accomplished with his blood. It would take only a moment, and surely Florian would be incensed were he to leave without investigation of the entire state of affairs. Why else would Florian have sent him here? For something as petty as a set of dinnerware?

Johann wound his way into the hall, which was decorated just as tastelessly as the sitting room. He could hear faint strains of conversation billowing up from the first floor, so he made sure to walk carefully on the balls of his feet. There was a door cracked an inch wide where the carpet ended, spilling light and the scent of rot into the rest of the house. Johann eased the door open with his palm and slipped in.

It was a guest room, the guest all trussed up in the four-poster bed, curtains drawn shut, incense burning at the four corners of the room as if that could mask the stench. Johann breathed it in: perfume, rot, body odor, and piss. No shit, though. Johann knew what a corpse smelt like, and what a corpse smelt like was a blood-logged ass soaking in the decayed offal matter of its last three meals.

He pulled the curtains open with a sprightly flick of the wrist.

"Rise and shine, Ambassador!"

The Ambassador did not respond. He had a fat hand clutched at the neck of his bedclothes. The sweat-stained cotton was a poor mask for his sickness. The dark plague blisters showed through the fabric, little black islands of disease scattered from his neck all the way down to his pelvis.

"Well, well, my darling dear did a real number on you, didn't he? Fucking look at you. Absolutely disgusting."

Johann made a clicking noise with his tongue. *That*

brought the Ambassador to his senses. He blinked his eyes open and turned his head to stare at Johann, glossy and half-present. There was already white filming over his sclera. His tongue was swollen up so big that it lolled out of his mouth. He moved his lips to no avail.

"Oh yes, my delicate snow-flower Florian fucked you up real good. I'm sure you heard all sorts of terrible things about what dwells in Norden, but you never thought you'd fall under the unforgiving eye of its avenging angel. I suppose it's only fair that I put you out of your misery."

It *was* only fair, to dole the duties out this way: for Johann to wipe away the refuse Florian cast behind him, to keep those dainty little hands unmarred by the scars he was raking into Elendhaven raw. Johann imagined himself as the shadow of death in the man's fraying sight. *No reason to be afraid*, Johann thought. *Death is kind. It's only life that holds suffering.* With infinite kindness, he climbed onto the bed with one knee and knelt at the Ambassador's side.

Understanding flooded the Ambassador's gaze. He began to struggle, but he was too bloated to turn over. Johann watched him, all his knives sheathed. Sure, it would be quick to slice him across the jugular, or pike him in the temple, but Johann was feeling magnanimous; he would send the poor sucker off sweetly.

Johann wrapped both hands around the Ambassador's tumid neck and didn't let go until he smelt shit.

*   *   *

He took a strip off the Ambassador's belly, and another off his back, where the boils were densest. He had to cut around the bedsores. He wrapped the meat up good and tight in three layers of perfumed silk before packing them in leather. Contemplating his work, he rolled the body back over and, on a whim, cut out the tongue. That he put in his pocket.

Florian was not impressed by this offering. "Why would you think I wanted this?" he demanded when he saw it, covering his mouth with a handkerchief.

"I thought you could use it as . . . research samples? To track the progress of the plague?"

"Johann, you don't . . . you don't understand *anything*." Florian sighed and ground his palm between his eyes. "You realize that you've just caused us more trouble?"

Johann rocked back and forth on his heels. "You know me, sweetheart. I live to serve."

Florian let out an ungraceful snort. His look of utter, familiar disdain was so pretty that Johann couldn't help but kiss him. Florian spun out of his grasp, horrified. "Don't touch me with that filth on your hands!"

"Fine," Johann sighed, and peeled off his gloves.

Florian really was as fragile as a new ice, but—

—the thing about newly frozen ice is that beneath it lurk dark shadows. Florian had darkness beneath his pale eyes all week. It was there when he took his morning coffee, when he gave counsel to the factory masters, when he pinched Johann's ear to make him sit still as he applied kohl and greasepaint to his translucent face.

For most people, a darkness behind the iris was a sign of melancholy. For Florian it bespoke pure elation. Thin ice isn't a problem for the sea; it's a problem for the blind idiot who steps out on it. The fool who breaks it gets sucked under; the ice, it mends.

Florian's eyes were full of drowned corpses as he and Johann dined once again with Ansley and his foreign business partner. In a locked smoking room, Florian daintily accepting a shisha pipe from Herr Charpentier. He took an exploratory puff and came up coughing, much to the delight of his companions.

Another man in the parlour was coughing, too. It was not from the smoke.

"A shame what happened to the Ambassador," said Ansley. He was chewing on a black cigar that stank of licorice, rolling it from one side of his mouth to the other while he talked, until he was surrounded on all sides by a fog of blue smoke. He folded open his gold-lined snuff case and offered it to Johann. "Smoke for your manservant?"

Florian covered the case with a tiny, soft hand. "Johann doesn't partake on the job."

Johann gave Florian a crisp smile and shoved him aside. "First time for everything, *Boss.*"

Florian puffed right up at the bold defiance, and Johann laughed with joy at being able to flirt under these starched-up bastards' noses. Half the men in the bar were closet buggerers anyway.

Johann leant down to light his cigar on the kerosene flame at the center of the table. A shadow crossed over him as he inhaled: Eleanor, coming to sit in their booth. She was stunning in a wheat-coloured brocade dress, lined from neck to ankle in hand-stitched doves. For once she was dressed as what she looked like: a girl from the colonies, rather than the Mittengelt nobility she pretended at. Her dark hair was pulled back in a thick braid that brushed her hip.

"May I have one as well, Ansley?" she asked, a hand at her collar and a quiver in her voice.

A shadow fell across Ansley's face as well. "Of course, my lady," he said, and moved aside to make space in the booth. She slid in like a fold in paper. There was a fragility about her that bled mourning from every gesture, as she smiled politely at each man in turn. Her gaze lingered on Florian, who, without missing a beat, tipped his head to her in courteous obeisance. But Johann could feel how tense he had gone.

Charpentier—in a show of drunken generosity—offered Eleanor the shisha pipe. Ansley and Florian had been calling him by his forename all night, cozy now that they'd shared a few drinks. Gillèrt, or Gillette, something like that. Maybe he hailed from Gillèrt? It didn't really matter; he wasn't long for the world. Johann did not miss the way he was sweating under his ruff. He'd spent the last two hours subtly tugging at his ascot, scratching the skin beneath his stylish muttonchops raw.

"Shisha, mademoiselle? You must be, ah, familiar with it, yes?"

Something dark flashed in Eleanor's eyes, a momentary crack in her mask. Thin ice, deep waters. Too fast for a lazy noble to catch. Johann cast a look at Florian to make sure he'd seen it. Florian watched her with a knuckle under his chin.

Eleanor giggled almost mechanically and dipped down to light her cigar. She said, "I've had shisha before, but I much prefer black tobacco." Johann caught her stumbling over her Mittengelt accent. Why the performance? He wondered who besides the Ambassador knew she was a Mage Hunter. His death might have left her all alone.

She breathed a smoke ring out from between her pursed lips like an expert. Ansley watched her with dark pupils blown out with lust. Well, that and the something extra laced into the shisha, some drug Charpentier had brought north with him. They were all feeling it by now.

"I am very sorry about—" Ansley coughed, adjusted his silk tie. The cigar made its journey to the other side of his mouth. "About what happened to the Ambassador. You two seemed . . . close."

Eleanor frowned the way she ought. She shuddered against the thought of savage things, the way she was supposed to. The cigar shook in her fingers, scattering ash across the table like the first flakes of a snowstorm. "It's not what you think," she whispered. "He was my . . . benefactor."

"I see! So this is how you speak the common tongue so well!" Charpentier beamed like he had just paid her a compliment. She bristled, almost imperceptibly.

"She speaks it better than you, certainly, Gilbert," Florian cut in, reaching for his drink. *Shit,* Johann thought, and adjusted his mental inventory of doomed businessmen. Florian took an impressive swig of his vodka bitters, then addressed Eleanor sympathetically. "It was really a terrible thing. Such an unusual murder, following his terrible illness . . . When I told you that you would see colours you'd never witnessed at home, I did not mean blood and blister. Truly, my heart goes out to you and yours."

Eleanor ducked her head. "Thank you, Herr Leickenbloom. It means much coming from you."

"I abhor the idea of a lady alone so far from home. Is there anything I can do for you?"

Eleanor looked up at Florian through her lashes. Her hair shadowed her face where the braid was loose. "Well . . . I'd heard," she said softly, tears at the corners of her eyes, "that your family, too, died of a plague."

Charpentier's and Ansley's heads spun together to gape at Florian. Johann kept looking at Eleanor. It occurred to him that Florian might have miscalculated—it was possible that the clever little lady knew exactly who she was looking for.

Florian's neutral expression strained at the edges. Johann could imagine how he'd look if he could: like he'd swallowed a spider. "Yes," he said, in a high, tinny voice. "That is true."

"Was it the same as the one that claimed my beloved benefactor?" she wondered, pressing the tips of her fingers to her bottom lip.

"My family passed when I was very young, so I could not possibly answer that question." Florian took a sip of his drink. There was nothing left in the glass but ice and lime. "Perhaps you can visit the town archives tomorrow and request the medical records, if you are so curious."

"I'm afraid that my education was not in the sciences, herr. Perhaps we could meet there and discuss this subject further."

"I regret that I have many appointments tomorrow. *Perhaps* you would deign to take my manservant with you. He does not look like much, but I assure you that he can read."

Charpentier shot a bushy-browed gape at Johann, shocked by this confident affirmation of peasant literacy.

Eleanor looked at Johann as well. *Really* looked at him, in the way few people did. Johann took a long drag off his cigar and hoped the smoke would help cloud her memory of their encounter at the beach. She pulled up and sighed into her own cig. "If it is all the same to you, I would rather not. It is improper, I think, for a lady to travel unaccompanied with a bandit, however reformed he may be."

Stalemate. Florian's cheeks were rosier than usual, and not from embarrassment.

"A bandit?" Ansley echoed, analyzing Johann from the corner of his vision.

"That's what Herr Leickenbloom told me," Eleanor said, eyes steady through the smoke. "At his party the other night. Correct?"

Florian picked at the lime in his glass. "You must be misremembering. I said that Johann was a cobbler."

"Is . . . is that so?" She blinked and scrunched up her nose, lost in the memory. "How strange . . . I recall the conversation rather vividly."

"Clearly," Florian sniffed, "you do not."

"Ah, enough of this!" Charpentier was swaying in his seat. He dug a cloth envelope out of his pocket and shook a handful of dried leaves onto the table. "Why is it that you are all so . . . so glum! Less talk of tragedy, more *shisha*!"

Ansley chuckled. "It's natural; tragedy is the culture of Elendhaven. One cannot help but be glum when he hardly sees the sun for half the year."

"I rather like our long winters," Florian said, head down, running a finger along the rim of his glass. "But then again, I am rather accustomed to them. My family could not afford to run south at the first sign of frost."

"Yes, but Elendhaven suits you, Herr Leickenbloom. You would detest Sandherst, I'd bet, let alone my family's villa on the southern coast."

Florian arched an eyebrow. "Why is that?"

"Well, for one thing"—Ansley tapped ash from his cigar—"the mines are open."

"You know, I have *heard*," Charpentier began, over-loud, breaking the tension with the grace of an avalanche, "that the people here say the end of the world will begin in this city. This, I think, is the most glum thing imaginable." He was picking freely at the boil on his neck now.

Florian was occupied still with Ansley's smug expression, so Johann spoke for him. "Actually," he said, reaching for the shisha pipe, "what *they* say is that the end of the world already began here. Hundreds of years ago."

"That's why the water is black, yes?" Eleanor asked with big, shocked eyes. Oh, she was good. Johann could see her effect, knew Ansley couldn't stand to have all her attention focused on other men. He finally peeled his eyes off Florian and pressed the last of his cigar into the marble ash bowl before gliding a few charming words in right under Charpentier's long red nose.

"In the age of sorcerers, they say a deadly spell split the silver mountain in two. It turned a thousand men and women to ash, and that ash snowed down all along the shore for ten days. When the ocean rushed in to fill the crater left by the spell, the water was black." He picked up his empty tumbler and held it to his eye, miming a spyglass. "If you stand on the cliffs outside the city, you can see the harbour is shaped like a crescent. That's how it earned its nickname—the Black Moon is the first sign of the end times in old barbarian myths."

"A rather leisurely apocalypse," Charpentier mused, "if it takes five hundred years."

Florian set his glass down. "It's only leisurely if you are tracking time on a calendar," he whispered. "The world is much, much older than we are, and the Gods older than that. The signs from the Allfather are meant to mirror an eclipse. First is the Black Moon. Second is a plague that will bring a long dark. The third is a war that will burn a circle around the oldest kingdoms of man. When our monuments are reduced to rubble, the Gods will ascend from the Black Moon and begin their final battle. Hallandrette is the watcher of that gate—the Allfather's favourite daughter. Our city's guardian."

"Is that why you love Elendhaven's long nights, Herr Leickenbloom?" Eleanor ventured softly. "Because of this myth that foretells such savage daylight?"

Florian shook his head and laughed. "Of course not. I'm a rational man. I believe what I see." He gestured towards the window. "And you can *see* clearly that the harbour is a volcanic crater; it was formed by geological forces, not mad sorcerers. But magic and war did poison this land, once. The allure of the story is obvious when you've lived here long enough. You feel it in every stone. In the way that the horizon bends over the ocean and disappears. In a certain sense, Elendhaven truly is the end of the world. After all, it dwells at the edge of the map."

A moment of reverent silence trailed Florian's speech.

In the booth behind them, two men discussed the market price of spider silk. On the other side of the parlour, the coughing man choked up his soup. The wind rattled the windows and sleet pelted against the slimy glass like a musket ball shattering bone.

Charpentier broke the silence, clapping a well-groomed hand on the table. "Brilliant!" he said as the glasses rattled. "*Glum*, but brilliant! How exciting, to live in a land of such sensational myths!"

Florian stared at Charpentier with an expression that could cut diamond.

"In the land where my mother was born"—Eleanor tapped the ash from her smoke into Ansley's bowl—"they believe that time is like a wheel, suspended from seven celestial chains. It's, er . . ." She let out a tired laugh and pretended to be abashed that all eyes were once again on her. "It's . . . complicated. I don't understand it all myself, but my mother told me that time is like a circle that we walk again and again. Everything that has happened has already happened, and will happen again."

"More exquisite words," bubbled Charpentier. He was punch-drunk, slumped in his seat so that his shoulder and Eleanor's met where the leather dipped. He picked up the end of her braid and began twirling it between his fingers. He giggled to himself, enchanted with how the hairs flopped and split as he spun it. She didn't say anything, but she did snatch it back when he tugged a bit too hard.

Ansley was enchanted not with her words, but with the slope of her neck. "Continue, my dear."

She set her cigar against the edge of the ash bowl and made a loop with her hands. Smoke spilt up around her and split where her thumbs joined. The lamplight made the smoke orange and her skin a sanguine gold. "We move through cycles that grow shorter with each rotation," she said, a melodic cadence to her words. "First is creation; then we prosper; then we preserve. Then, decline. Finally, decay. The last cycle is a corrupted world, so far from the light. When this cycle collapses, the world folds in on itself. And then, we begin again."

"'A corrupted world'?" Ansley gave a snort and polished off his ale. "Like this one, in which Ambassadors are carved up by some pervert even as they stare down the angel of death?"

"Oh, of course we are living in the last cycle." Eleanor set her hands down. Retrieved her cigar. "Of that my mother's people have no doubt."

"In that case," Florian said, eyes fixed on the flame at the center of the table, "there's nothing to fear from the end of the world. Annihilation is a fire that cleanses what it burns. For a corrupted world, apocalypse is the only hope for redemption."

Johann studied his master's cherubic profile. *Don't you feel it, sometimes? As if the world wants to consume itself.* Florian's own eyes were consumed by the flame's light. It flickered beneath his gaze and flashed blue.

"That's one way of looking at it, I suppose," Eleanor replied, trailing smoke through the air as she leant forward.

"But do you believe it, Lady Eleanor?" Florian asked very carefully.

Eleanor's response was calculated in its tactlessness. She dashed her cigar out on the tablecloth and said, "Goodness me, of course not!"

* * *

"How asinine!" said Florian when he and Johann were alone. The streets were dark and deep, all the mud turned up by the melting snow. Florian stumbled as he walked, unsteady from too much drink and drug. He slipped on a patch of black ice and Johann caught him by the elbow, tucked him under his arm. Florian balked at the contact but did not struggle. There was no one to see them stroll so close. They were taking a route home through the abandoned textile district. Florian despised the shorter path through the city squares packed with the working-class lushes out in full force, and the carriages they could have hailed were occupied by the one thing he hated more: the monied drunks.

The storm had passed. Above them, the moon scattered diffuse light through the crumbling clouds. It made a tattered canvas of the burnt-out factories that lined the streets. As they passed beneath the skeleton of the one Florian had taken Johann to the day they met, where they had first tested his "skills," Johann wondered if it was the textile mill that Florian's family had once owned, the one where Daddy Leickenbloom had contracted the plague by playing pretend that he was generous.

"She knows," Johann said. "That you're a sorcerer, I mean."

"Oh yes, yes." Florian waved the words off. "That's a problem for tomorrow. Right now, I'm drunk."

"Aren't you worried she's going to break our door down in the middle of night?"

"No. I'm not some common hedge witch. Mage Hunters like to have probable cause before they go storming into an important man's home with their pistols drawn. She'll go to the archives first, look up whatever it is she wants to know about my family and the plague. Of course, she won't find anything, which will stall the investigation. Anyway—" Florian hooked his hand around Johann's elbow. "Did you see the way Ansley and Gilbert were enthralled by that woman's fairy tale? Are their lives so stale

that they slobber at the bit for stories of doom and de-
struction?"

Johann smiled at Florian's drunken lack of inhibition.
Sober, he would not be caught dead gossiping. "Did *you*
notice how the ponce asked six whole times about the
state of the Ambassador's body?"

"Absurd."

"I almost told him. Think he would have been so curious if he knew the man shit liquid when the lights went
out?"

Florian snickered and leant his cheek against Johann's
rib cage for a moment. Johann thought he was snuggling
for warmth, but it turned out that he was just blowing his
nose. He pulled free of the half embrace and went stag-
gering into the street, spinning around with his arms out.

"What a thing it is, to see men *hunger* for the end
times!"

"Heh. Little did they know that they were sitting right
beside their imagined apocalypse. Snug with its harbin-
ger, letting him suck down their shisha and paying for
his drinks."

Florian reeled to a stop and his amusement turned to
disgust. "That's the problem, isn't it? Unwise to dream of
death in a world where someone has the power to make
those dreams come true."

There he was: pale and small in the moonlight, smaller

even in his fur-lined coat—precisely tailored, tucked at the waist, and bulky beneath the elbows where his mittens pushed against the cuffs. A pinprick of light in a dark winter sky, the nexus around which Elendhaven's universe revolved. How could this friable child hold the future in his horrible hands?

"Hmm." Johann snaked his hands out of his pockets and sauntered up to him. "Right now, I bet you could make my dreams come true, too."

Florian sighed. "Has that line netted you success in the past?"

"Nah," said Johann. "But this usually works."

He pushed Florian down with a sharp palm to the breastbone. Florian's shoes were impractical: cloth showpieces with ribbons on the ankles and wooden heels. They skidded through the mud so smoothly that he made almost no noise when he landed, elbows first, in the gutter. His head bounced off the spongy ground and then he lay still, breathing loud and trembling with silent fury. Johann was on him like a blanket a moment after, the tails of his unbuttoned coat flapping loud as bat wings. He grinned down at Florian, who was lost beneath blue shadows.

"Get off of me," Florian said quietly.

"I'm always the one getting my hands dirty, buttercup," Johann purred, drawing a lock of Florian's wheat-hair up between thumb and forefinger. It fell away streaked with mud. "But I think we both belong down in the gutter, don't you?"

Florian watched his hair fall. It hit his cheek and smeared the rouged skin. Johann popped open the first three buttons of Florian's coat and smoothed a hand over the silk shirt underneath. Ah, there it was: a humming-bird heartbeat.

"Don't," said Florian into Johann's mouth. "Don't," said the way his arms flew up to bat against Johann's chest. Johann laughed into the kiss, imagined himself and Florian sinking beneath the mud so that it filled their mouths and their eyes. Such a thing would not kill Johann, but it might be nice to stay that way for a while— until the spring came to melt the top layer of frost-glaze and flowers grew from Florian's rib cage. A wedding, of sorts.

Florian bit down on Johann's lips. Not hard enough to draw blood, *adorable*. Johann drew back to mock him, but he found that when he did he was not moving of his own accord. He flew back, propelled by Florian's magic in his marrow. Florian was furious in the mud. Piping mad, practically steaming from the ears. In fact, the ground was steaming around him. In a circle tens of feet wide, the frost had melted and the grass was catching green flame at the tips.

"Do you like it when I do this? Is that it?" Florian demanded. Johann could not nod, or shake his head. He was not sure which would emerge if he had control of his body. He had not been puppeteered gently; his spine was over-cocked and his arms pulled back at an impossible angle. The pain was exquisite.

Florian stumbled to his feet and tried to wipe the mud off his coat but succeeded only in dirtying his goat-wool mittens. "Look what you've done. My outfit is ruined."

"Well," Johann choked out. "At least it's not one . . . of your better ones. . . ."

Florian was struck silent by that comment. Johann could have sworn that he almost smiled. At the very least, he let Johann's limbs go free.

"You're impossible. Why should I expect that you would ever learn a single lesson?" He sighed, then flicked his wrist to force Johann to scoop him up bridal-style. Florian released his magical hold and flourished his hands, gesturing with drunken certainty in the direction of the Leickenbloom mansion.

"Now, manservant, you may take me home."

"It is a credit to me as a 'bodyguard' that I don't drop you right back in the mud, Boss."

"Don't call me that."

"*Sweetheart.*"

"Or that."

Is this it? Johann wondered. *The longer fall I was look-ing for? To know that I was summoned up from the dark ether to do a monster's deeds for Hallandrette's truest son?*

And when our work is done, I will carry him to the bot-tom of the sea, where we both belong. Deep beneath the silt our bones will turn to salt.

* * *

There was a memory that Florian did not dredge up often. He pushed it down, down, down, as far as it would go. It came back sometimes in pieces of jagged, visceral sensation. The sting of the sea breeze against his cheeks. The sound of a body consumed by the sea. The coarseness of Flora's winter coat under his bare hands.

Flora said, "But what if you threw someone in?"

Flora said, "But what if they weren't dead yet? They'd come back all mutated and strange."

Flora said, "Florian, don't you want to know?"

She was joking; she really was. The boy at the docks, he didn't know what to think about a tiny girl with sun-coloured hair and a fur coat asking to see his paring knife and then holding it to his neck. He was bigger than her, dark hair and dark eyes. No mother or father, just a knife, and a couple of coins in his pocket. She was so bold it scared him to shaking.

She wasn't laughing when he slipped and hit his head on

a rock. His blood was black under the moonlight. Florian thought he might have still been breathing when they hauled him off the dock.

But Flora said, "Now that it's done, we might as well find out."

– VIII –

HALLANDRETTE'S SON

Johann awoke to the sight of Florian sitting at his mirror, covering his bruises with thick whitening paste. He mixed his own greasepaint: sweetened vinegar, chalk, goat fat, and a touch of pink paint. All the ingredients were imported.

"I have a job for you," Florian said, not looking up from his work. Johann rolled out of bed and came to set a hand on Florian's hair. Their eyes met in the mirror.

"The Mage Hunter, right? You want me to—" Johann did his favourite knifey gesture.

Florian pressed his eyes shut and pinched the bridge of his nose. "I'd prefer—in *general*—that you treat that as a last resort, rather than a first."

"I don't know, Florian, this whole situation seems pretty 'last resort' to me. What do you expect me to do otherwise? Seduce her?"

Florian scrunched up his nose and dabbed a drop of greasepaint beneath one eye. "Of course not."

Johann grinned wide and slow, walking two fingers up the curve of Florian's back. "It's not undoable, you know. I can be charming when I want to be. I could play the humble cobbler, show her around the city, make her laugh. Bring her back here so you can work your magic . . ."

Florian shivered. "Don't even joke." He lowered his eyes to examine his large set of cheek rouges. His eyelashes were so long, like blades of spelt after they were shorn of chaff. "Besides, I'll be in meetings late into the evening."

Johann rolled his finger over the bumps in Florian's spine where it dipped beneath his hair. He had a scattering of pockmarked scars there, and beneath his collarbones as well. Not from plague boils, but pox sores. It seemed obvious that Florian should have been an ill child: no wonder he was so slight and circumspect. There was a sick joke lurking in the air about a boy so often ill being the sole member of his household passed over by the plague. If Johann were not so terribly besotted by the noises Florian made when kissed beneath the jugular he would have voiced it out loud.

"I made tea," Florian said suddenly.

Johann straightened as Florian handed him one of the silver cups recently liberated from Ansley's manor. He sniffed it and smelt dates. "What *is* this?"

"A gift from Gilbert. He thinks to butter me up with sweets if he cannot do it with sums."

Johann took a sip and wrinkled his nose. It was sickeningly sweet. "Cute. He'll be dead within the week."

"Yes. He must have contracted the Ambassador's illness. I'd not expected it to spread so fast."

Johann raised the cup to the light, turned it to examine the engravings. Snow orchids, with lines of verse cleaving through the petals. It took him a moment to realize the arched handwriting was in the common alphabet—the lines were written in complete gibberish.

Oh. Of course. *I've identified the cipher, but I'm missing all the keys,* Florian said. Perhaps Grandmama Leickenbloom had not been as senile as Florian thought, to have kept these out of his reach.

"Florian," Johann began, remembering something. "Is this the . . . first time you've done this?"

Florian's hand stilled where it was applying rogue.

Johann continued: "When I was at the sick house, I overheard the Ambassador talking about his aides falling ill. *Permanently* ill."

"Ah." Florian fluffed his brush in a darker shade of powder. "I hadn't realized that they died."

"You scolded me for being hasty with the Ambassador, but you haven't been careful, either."

Florian shot him a withering gaze in the mirror. "Obviously this isn't the first time I've attempted to deploy the plague. I've been occupied with this venture for almost half as long as I've been alive. It's my life's work, my life. Johann, what do you even care if I've done this before?"

"I *don't* care. I just—" Something crawled down Johann's throat and gripped him tight. For some reason, his next words felt like speaking through tar. "Are you . . . ever going to explain to me what that is?" His mouth was dry. Stripped of his artifice, he sounded young. What the *fuck*. "Your life's work? Your end goal?"

Florian spun his chair around and smiled up at Johann: the expression was economical, but genuine mischief sparkled in his eyes. There was still mud in his hair.

"Why should I? It's not as if you're ever going to tell me no."

* * *

Johann shadowed Eleanor all day. He acquainted himself with his old friends: roofs, eaves, alleys, gutters. Did what he used to do for lunch and swiped an oyster roll from a man who forgot about him in the time it took his mouth to form the word *thief*. The shadows embraced him, and the citizens ignored him, letting him trail his target with barely a care. This was the Elendhaven he remembered: orphans and prostitutes and hostel owners who watered their ale and hit their children where everyone could see it.

Eleanor's disguise was almost as good as his. He'd watched her leave the suite that morning in her plain leather duster and her un-whitened skin. She almost slammed into Ansley in the street and he rebuffed her cruelly, as a stranger, without even looking at her face. She had to grab him by the arm to get his attention. Johann slinked along the rooftops to follow them to the alleyway where he watched them quarrel, too high to hear the specifics. Ansley raised a hand to smack her, but she caught his wrist. He left, harried and quick footed, when he saw the bandolier beneath her jacket.

After that, she began to ask questions about the plague. She began to ask the right people, too: the innkeepers, the fishermen, the *cobblers.* Cleverer and cleverer, thought Johann, this thin-handed, long-legged huntress. She knew that Elendhaven's elite were a dead end, and that whoever made it that way had likely not stopped to look *down.*

Johann decided to give her a good knifing before she even entered the archives, no matter what Florian wanted. She emerged with a thin sheaf of paper under one arm, but, unexpectedly, she did not head for Florian's manor. Instead—just as the sky began to turn pink—she went to the shore. Johann stood for a while in her long shadow, watching her watch the sun go down. She sat on a piece of driftwood, her feet lost in the hair-tangle of white weeds that surrounded it. Quietly, Johann came up behind her and saw that, once again, she had a white stone in her palm.

"Throw it against the cliff, and the thing you love most will come back to you," Johann said, chin close to her shoulder.

She did not startle. "I've heard that myth somewhere," she said softly. "That these are eggs laid from the mouth of the goddess Hallandrette, that they awaken when filled with tragedy."

"They're Elendhaven's answer to death. No unjust passing goes unpunished here at the edge of the earth."

Still not looking at him, Eleanor rolled the stone down her fingers and held it up against the sunset. "My mother's people do not believe in death," she said. "Not true death, anyway. They believe that people live many times, always learning, always forgetting."

"'Everything that has happened has already happened, and will happen again,'" Johann quoted, sauntering around the log so that he was blocking her light. He smiled down at her, wolfish and charming. "Have we spoken before?"

She narrowed her eyes. The stone went in her pocket, and her braid went over her shoulder. "The man who told me the myth. You introduced yourself as Elendhaven."

Johann's knife itched against his wrist. "You remember, then."

"I thought it was a dream. I've had many strange dreams since coming to this terrible city." The look on her face said that she was still dreaming, all liquid and clouds. "What's your real name, Mister Elendhaven?"

What's a name? "Johann."

She smiled and offered a narrow hand. "Mine is Kanya."

Oh ho. "That's not the name I've heard whispered among the parlour shadows." Instead of shaking her hand, he slid his fingers under her chin.

"You are the only man in this city who has not lied to me yet."

She was entranced by him, like a mouse taken in by a snake. Was this an effect of his aberrant nature? A siren song that rose up from his pheromones and unlocked the secret desires of humans who spent too long in his shadow? He'd never really thought about it—the way people talked to themselves when looking at him. Every person he'd ever killed had *thirsted* for it. Every human had a desperate void churning inside them. The world wants to devour itself, Florian said.

This is going to be so easy it's practically criminal, he thought to himself. Holding back laughter hurt bone deep. He shucked a knife from his sleeve, and she whispered, "Your master, on the other hand . . ."

Johann was not shocked. He was nothing at all. He kept hold of her chin, his grip turning from gentle to severe. She showed no pain. When Johann reared back to stare at her, her eyes were dark pools deep as the ocean where Hallandrette waited for the end of the world. Hadn't she said that the water was clear in the land where she was born?

"That was a very stupid thing you just said," Johann told her.

"And it is a stupid thing your master has done, placing his servant in view of a Mage Hunter. This is the mistake sorcerers always make, summoning things up from the depths, parading them around in front of strangers, always so certain they're ten steps ahead. In the right hands, cannot magic do anything?"

"Is that how you were able to finally recognize me?"

Kanya ghosted a finger down the hollow of her throat. "There is a tonic we drink. Mercury and silver. It makes for a short career, but"—she wrapped her hand around his wrist and wrenched it until the knife came loose—"a high enough dose makes magic flow harmlessly through you."

Johann yanked his arm free, surprised at her strength. His blade clattered on the hard sand, then disappeared beneath her foot. "Did you suspect Florian this whole time?"

She shook her head. "I should have, but there were extenuating circumstances. I was sent by the Crown to investigate a series of rather odd deaths. *Ansley*, however, issued a contract against your master some months ago. He had no proof, and to be honest, I do not think that he believes Herr Leickenbloom is a sorcerer. What he *does* believe is that he will do everything in his power to stymie his business prospects. The first thing I heard when I entered the city was this petty feuding over the railroad, and so I dismissed his complaints entirely."

"It took that little to throw you off the mark?" Johann laughed, easing back on his heels. "No offense, miss, but you're a bit shit at your job."

"It wasn't only that," Kanya admitted, with an admirable humility. "You must give your master more credit. It's only very recently that he's gotten sloppy. His work mendaciously adjusting his family's records is subtle and extremely thorough. I went and looked at the city's medical documents a second time, just like he suggested. They were curiously trim for a family with such deep roots in the city. But words are easily manipulated. History lives on in other ways." She dipped a hand into her pocket and produced a slim ring box. She traced her finger along the silver casing, and Johann could see clearly that it bore the Leickenbloom family seal.

Shit.

"What I *did* find in the archives were records of Ansley's father obtaining many of the Leickenblooms' antiques in an auction nearly twenty years ago. Once I knew to look, I saw this symbol everywhere in Ansley's manor. It's the same one your master wears on his left hand. This box looks to have been passed down several generations." She popped it open to show the inscription under the lid: names, with dates carved beside them. "Aloysia, to Odette, to Magdela, to Flora. That last one— she was born the same year as Florian Leickenbloom, but there was no mention of her in the medical records. I thought, why is it that no one remembers that the Leickenblooms had two children?"

Johann said nothing. He sized her up, slid a hand into his pocket where the railroad spike was still rusting away.

"Johann." She sounded so *empathetic*. Adorable. "There is a reason I wanted to know the whole story. Whatever Herr Leickenbloom has put into your head about me, Mage Hunters do not execute without ample *reason*. This doesn't have to end with your master shot dead. But it *does* have to end. You know it must."

"Yeah." Johann sighed. "You're right. I guess we'll have to do this the hard way."

He knocked her down with a heel to the stomach. She did not absorb the blow with grace but toppled back to the rocky ground, her legs spread-eagle with knees still hooked over the log. Johann fell upon her. He wrested her hands from her bandolier and tried to pin them against the ground. She bucked him off with a knee to the bladder, but he kept hold of her coat lapel. The weight of his body yanked her off balance and sent them rolling over each other in the sand. This time when he pinned her down, he did it with his forearm to her jugular.

Oh, she struggled. Valiantly, *heroically*. It had been a long time since Johann had wrestled with something that wanted to live. It was infuriating and exhilarating to feel every part of her body fight him down to the blood. Johann drank the fear in her eyes like it was two-hundred-mark brandy. He wasn't choking her hard enough to kill, just enough that she'd be placid when he drove the spike into her eye. He choked her until her vision went wide, until he saw that animalistic, *euphoric* frequency reflected back at him in her shuddering sclera; the chasm that howled in the space between life and death, where creatures lost their names.

"If you stop *struggling,*" he purred, "I'll gut your brain in one stroke, sweet and short like a surgeon does."

He reached into his pocket and found it empty. The shock was enough to still him, a fatal pause. He'd underestimated the determination of a half-dead woman with substantial martial training. Or perhaps he'd grown used to Florian's performative struggle, so drunk on the hedonistic allure of violence as play he'd forgotten how to listen to his instincts. He'd forgotten to watch Kanya's hands. She fought space between them and rammed the rail spike into his larynx.

Johann's vision swam, red and blurry at the edges. He let Kanya go, stumbled back, tripped over the log. *Stupid, stupid.* The tide was coming in behind him, lapping at the shoreline with its greedy tongue. He rose, bleeding from the neck and still laughing, a terrible, guttural sound. She was shards of black and red against the horizon as she raised her pistol and fired.

* * *

By necessity, his revenge began slow.

Florian lived alone in a house full of corpses for two months. He became used to them: to the smell and the bloat, to the rot and the strange colours a human being turned when there was no soul inside of them. He no longer wanted to be a doctor.

The first man he practised wizard's tricks on was his father's accountant. A minor noble in his own right, and a distant cousin of the Leickenblooms through marriage on his mother's side. Unlike the Leickenblooms proper, he had money.

"It says here in my father's will that you were to be my benefactor were anything to befall him," Florian said, watching the accountant's eyes glaze over. It was a lie, but Florian found that if he lied in a certain cadence of voice while twisting his thumb white, people believed him.

Every night he went to the shoreline, a roe in his pocket. So many people were throwing their dead into the harbour that the far end of the Black Moon was thick with their refuse: cracked spectacles, splintered ribs, shoes with the feet still in them, jewelry made blue by the water. No Flora. Not even the ribbons she wore in her hair. Not even her family ring, a perfect twin to the one Florian still wore.

This is what Florian found instead: a boy with black hair, black eyes, clothes ripped by the tide, pale skin with no incisions. A thread of seaweed behind his ear. A face Florian knew and had not wanted to see again.

Breathing.

He poked the boy with a stick to make sure that the rise

and fall of his chest was not just nerve endings sending instinctual signals through the chest, like a chicken twitching after its head's been chopped off. Slowly, like rising from a dream, the boy nudged his elbows beneath him. It hitched up and opened his eyes, one at a time. It stared at Florian in the wash of blue moonlight.

"What am I?" it asked.

Florian dropped the stick and ran, the rock burning a hole in his pocket. He locked all the shutters when he got home and spent all night locked in his bedroom, holding his knees. That cruel lady, the goddess Hallandrette. She had sent him the wrong gift.

The boy was gone the next morning. Florian resolved to never think of it again, but he held on to the hallanroe he'd fetched for Flora. He sewed it into the lining of his mother's favourite coat.

* * *

The monster awoke in pieces, dreams rising like steam from the sewers on a warm spring morning. Memories scattered, glass on the floor. It had to put them together, find the right shape.

A corpse spit up on the tide, caught on the rocks by a fold of skin. Sitting up in the pale moonlight, what is a moon? What is the sea? What is a name? A little Hans, a little Ralf.

Little wee dock rat? A spit of a hallankind? Lessons from a large stone. Falling, like a crow with clipped wings, a crash that wants to swallow you whole. What am I, what am I, who—

A shadow in Elendhaven's gutter. A name said in a certain tone of voice. That's what makes a thing real. Skin that glows like the part of an insect under the exoskeleton. Hands that do terrible things, work that needs to be done. A hallway that you cannot take another step forward in.

When it's over, a hallankind must return to the sea where I will sit beneath the silt until my bones turn to salt. A little Hans. A little Ralf. Wee little Johann.

Johann—

Johann whipped upright, delirious, head out of order. The sun was a line shimmering on the sea. He turned to see a halo of blood and bone in the sand. Mushy pink puddles, a single eye bounced out to sit alone among the cracked seashells. He ground the heel of his hand into his socket, pressed against the searing pain of nerves growing back. She'd burst his head like a rotten apple felled from the tree.

"Bitch is a good shot," Johann heard himself mutter. His voice was still cracked from the stained spike at his feet. His thoughts, soggy. There was somewhere he needed to be. Something he needed to do. Someone he—

"Shit," Johann said as he staggered to his feet. He said

it all the way back up the craggy path to the mansion. He yelled it when he slammed through the door.

"*Shit,* Florian, we gotta go. And I really mean it this ti . . ."

Johann trailed off. He saw Florian seated on the chartreuse love seat in the sitting room, holding a cup of tea. He looked very put together all things considered, but Johann heard the cup shaking against its saucer, rattled by his fingers. Johann noticed that there was a second cup set out on the center table, half-drained.

"You might have deferred to your first resort after all. I'd not thought the situation this dire."

Kanya stepped out from the shadows. Her jacket was buttoned over the bruise Johann had left on her throat. She raised her gun and leveled the muzzle at Johann. To Florian, she said:

"Undo him."

Florian's laugh was curdled. "You might as well ask me to sink Elendhaven into the sea."

Kanya let out a sad, thin breath. "I understand that you are a damaged man, Herr Leickenbloom. I too am an orphan, raised in a city that hated me. A land that I hated. You—"

Florian cut her off sharply. "Do not try to reason with me, Mage Hunter. You don't know anything about my life, or what I've done."

"Herr Leickenbloom, I am not a cruel woman." Kanya stepped behind the couch, her eyes trained on Johann's face. "I do not wish all sorcerers dead. In Mittengelt . . . in the city where I was trained, there is a treatment. You could be saved."

"A treatment?" Florian echoed. "I have heard of this *treatment*. They shove a pike up your left nostril and stir it about until they find the part of your brain that scholars say creates magic. But I know better: magic is not in the brain, miss; it is in the *bones*. I would sooner die."

"Is that really what you want?" she asked sadly. *Pityingly.*

Florian closed his eyes and took a sip of his tea. "At this point, it does not matter one way or the other."

It mattered to Johann. He almost didn't feel it, his hand sliding beneath his jacket to snatch out a knife. He threw it on instinct. His nerves moved faster than his brain. But it was not Florian's power that moved him—it was something deep in Johann's marrow, a tug like the moon pulling the ocean home.

The blade skimmed Kanya's left arm, put her pistol off target. Johann leapt the couch and rushed her, taking her to the floor. Florian was caught out and spilt his tea all over himself as he jumped to his feet. Kanya and Johann struggled for a few seconds, primal and desperate, as if answering an aching want left over from their spat at the beach. Kanya rolled them over and slammed his skull into the floor by the hair as Johann scratched at her face with both hands. She staggered to her feet and he grabbed after her, twisting her against his chest. She jerked an elbow back against him, but he had an arm locked around her stomach. She bit his wrist the first time he tried to wrap fingers around her neck. The second time, he forced a knife to her throat, but not before she found her pistol. They swayed together, stalemated: his blade at her jugular, her weapon on his master, who was frozen pale with a tipped teacup in one hand and his hair askew. Florian, who controlled Johann like a puppet, who had the whole city dancing to his tune, confronted with something as simple as a gun all he could do was gape.

"Let me go, or I'll kill him," she gasped.

"That'd be a poetic way to sign your own death warrant."

"You bluff with confidence, Herr Johann, but I'm not afraid of you. I know what you are."

"And what, exactly, do you think I am?" Johann hissed in her ear.

"A homunculus of some sort," Kanya answered, voice steady with the surety of absolute faith. "You're born of his blood, and controlled by it. When he dies, so will you."

Johann was too slow to stop the shot. The jerk of his elbow knocked it off course by a head and a half. Florian was hit in the gut. His pale eyes fluttered open as the round blew open his stomach. He wobbled on his feet, then collapsed in a crumble of silks and gold and unbrushed yellow hair. He scattered the tea table's burntdown candles, its little plates, its lace cup-setters. The metal teapot hit the floor with a hollow clang.

"Bad bet, lady," Johann snarled, and slit Kanya's throat. She went down like a gutted fish, boneless and bloody, making a horrible sound from the hole in her neck.

She was dying quick, but not quick enough for Johann, who followed up on his work by setting a heel on her throat until she stopped twitching and lay still. At the front end of the sitting room, the curtains were pulled open an inch. A beam of red light cut through, collecting dust glimmer. It fell across where Florian was laid in a plashet of his own blood, surrounded by broken china and wax.

Johann knelt at his master's side. His edges still felt light, undefined. Blurry where his eye hadn't completely healed. What to do when he was dead? Where to go? Should he crawl back into the sea? Drag Elendhaven there with him, like an anchor over his shoulder? What was Elendhaven without Florian? A foul spit of land sinking deeper into the sediment every day. What was Johann without Florian? A name that no one knew.

Who would ever have thought that a thing, once named and held in open palm, would want to curl up and stay there forever? Johann stroked a hand down Florian's side to feel where his guts were loose and spilling out onto the floor. It was hard to believe it came out of him, the same slippery meat that was stuffed inside everyone else. He pulled off both of his gloves and took Florian's hand in his bare palms. "Florian, this . . . this is a stupid way to die."

Florian struggled to speak, but there was blood in his mouth. Johann gripped his hand harder.

"After all that, you can't intend to actually *die*."

"Goddess . . . Johann . . . sh-sh. . . . shut up. . . ." Florian coughed up blood all over his chin, over his collar where mud had been streaked the night before. "There is . . . still one thing I need you . . . to do. C-come closer."

Johann obeyed. What else could he do? Florian set his free palm on his forehead. It was fever warm.

"If . . . a rejected gift comes back to you . . . when you most need it, wouldn't it be blasphemous . . . to refuse it again?"

"I don't understand," Johann said, but he did. Not in his head, but somewhere deeper. He understood it in his *bones,* a stone kept in a lonely boy's pocket, a toy that cannot be broken. Florian probably waited all these years for Hallandrette to send his sister back to him, but here was Johann. And here was Florian. It had to mean something. To Johann, it meant everything.

Florian's veins began to glow, bright through the sheer fabric of his tunic. The monster felt his memories come loose under the sorcerer's beautiful, smooth palm, easy as a tooth unhinged at the root. The glass of his mind flew apart at the cracks and the pieces were sucked under the water, taken by the tides to wash up on distant shores. He would never know their names.

Blue-lipped and shivering, Florian whispered, "A hallankind exists to make its master's dreams come true. S-so go forth . . . and do that. . . ."

– IX –

JOHN

For a long time, he didn't have a name. What he had were long fingers that knew the grip of a knife and a face that drew victims in. What he had were eyes that remembered streets, feet that knew gutters, palms that creaked in leather gloves and forgot the stain of blood easily.

He got his name from the coroner who looked over his body: "Another John Doe. Washed up on shore, lungs crushed under the water. Boils found beneath the armpits, but no signs of internal hemorrhage. Probable cause of death: drowning."

A lovely gift from a dead man. John made sure the coroner died the moment the knife went in him. A clean death. John needed his clothes.

It was not safe to stay in Elendhaven. A constable had seen his face and remembered it well enough to draw a facsimile. The moment John saw his sharp nose and long chin on a poster he put his affairs in order and stole a train ticket south. Elendhaven was not long for the world besides; there was a plague tickling the borders of the city and word was no doctor could find a cure. It followed John through the city's guts, taking those his knife passed over. "Magical," they whispered. A month back there was a queer death on the edge of town. A Mage Hunter turned up dead in the home of Herr Florian Leickenbloom. Her body was a whole room's length away from the dead dandy, her throat mysteriously crushed. They whispered that the Leickenblooms had cursed them again. Any day now the whole city was going to fall into the ocean.

Anyway, there was more fun to be had in Mittengelt. Sandherst was a city bigger than Elendhaven by more than five counts, and an easy reach by train. John eavesdropped on the Mitten folk beside him as he watched the countryside clip by in blinkered still shots through the cabin window.

"—removed her womb and took it with him. That was, it says, after cutting her right up along the insides of her thighs."

"That's the third one this month! What else was done to her?"

"Just that. It's not like the last one. . . ."

"Oh, that ghastly business with her face . . . cut her lips off in two pieces. What do you think he means by all this, the murderer?"

"I don't think it means a thing. It's the *age* that we live in. Those poor dears . . . they were in the wrong place at the wrong time, that's for sure."

A pause in conversation, and then: "Do you think this will be the last one?"

John had to bury his face in his coat to keep from laughing. What self-absorbed idiots, he thought, so *bored* with their lives that they hungered for news of mutilated women. Unwise to dream of death in a world where someone has the power to make those dreams come true. You never knew when the man sitting next to you on the train was an honest-to-god *monster*.

At the station, John was stopped by the ticket master. "I'm sorry, I don't remember you getting on. May I see your ticket, please?"

John did not have one. He'd gotten on legally in Elendhaven but jumped the connection when the security wasn't looking. He shot the man his biggest, sharkiest grin and slapped him on the shoulder. "Don't worry about it," he said.

The ticket master got an odd look on his face, all watery and half-asleep.

"Go on ahead," he murmured, eyes sliding right off John. Ah, that was more like it.

As John jumped the gap to the platform, he heard one of the passengers behind him begin coughing. He took a deep breath of Sandherst air: it was crisp and smoky, filled with steam and noise. It was nothing like Elendhaven, this city with wide streets and sandstone buildings and fountains that spit up clear water. The train station was bustling with hundreds of people from all walks of life: cottons to silks, silver changing hands, middle-class women with smartly dressed children waddling after them like a line of ducklings. Oh yes, there was mischief to be done.

Whistling to himself, John put his hands in his pockets and disappeared into the crowd.